TIFFANY TURNER

The Lost Secret of the Green Man

of the

The Crystal Keeper Chronicles

BOOK II

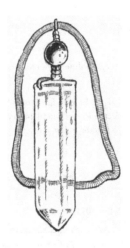

COVER ART AND ILLUSTRATION BY RICH WALLACE

Order this book online at www.trafford.com
or email orders@trafford.com

Most Trafford titles are also available at major online book retailers.

Printed in Victoria, BC, Canada.

ISBN: 978-1-4269-2156-8 (sc)
ISBN: 978-1-4269-2157-5 (hc)

Library of Congress Control Number: 2009940713

*Our mission is to efficiently provide the world's finest, most comprehensive book publishing
service, enabling every author to experience success. To find out how to publish your book, your
way, and have it available worldwide, visit us online at www.trafford.com*

Trafford rev. 12/14/09

www.trafford.com

North America & international
toll-free: 1 888 232 4444 (USA & Canada)
phone: 250 383 6864 ♦ fax: 812 355 4082

Dedicated to my husband and family that support me, my friends that have heard all the ideas and said, "Go for it", and to my students, that are my inspiration.

Contents

Prologue

Rupert entered through the oak tree's rounded door. He spotted Castrotomas staring into his far-seeing crystal. It began to grow cloudy as Castro's tail swished back and forth. Rupert's grey tabby fur was full of dust and small twigs. His master was a cat who focused heavily on his work. And what was before him was an important matter. Castrotomas hadn't torn away from the seeing crystal in two days. Small bowls of food stood uneaten. The workshop within the oak tree was cluttered with books, notes, and leaves.

Rupert looked over at his Master's meals. It was a shame to waste such good fish and fowl. He sighed as he looked around the workshop. It was his chore to keep things tidy being the Master's apprentice. When Castrotomas didn't eat, it made his job harder. There wasn't much else to do when Castrotomas was engrossed in his work.

Rupert moved over to interrupt Castro. When Castro forgot to eat, the only thing that Rupert could do was pester. It sometimes worked to howl once or twice to get his attention.

"Master, you forgot to eat again." Rupert tried to hide the irritation.

Humph. "Don't bother me unless you have something that is important to your studies." Castrotomas didn't look away from the crystal, but swished his tail in a twitch-like fashion.

"Master, is there anything more on the flow of energy and did you eat anything today?" Rupert turned his golden eyes to look expectantly. There was no answer. He was feeling a need to howl when he noticed the swirls in the far-seeing crystal start to slow. The rounded shape took on a green glow.

"There." A whisper escaped Castro's lips. "A small opening in the flow of energy. "It's as if..." Castro pulled back his whiskers. "It is being drained for some purpose."

"But to where Master?" Rupert put a paw forward, the fight over eating forgotten.

"I know not, but we may find out all too soon. The shadow is growing day by day. Ever since the Shadow Sorcerer, Balkazaar, escaped his bonds I have noticed a change in the flow of energy. It could be him affecting the flow of energy in the World of Fairy and with the humans. But unless I can see some source connecting the two, I will not know."

"What can we do Master?" Rupert's fur started to bristle.

"There is nothing to do but wait. I've been watching the training of one promising Crystal Keeper. Her name is Wanda. She was made a Crystal Keeper in the World of Fairy in the Western Realms. Her training has progressed well this summer.

She has already faced a trap by Balkazaar. She had to face her Crystal Keeper challenge unaided in a shadow trap maze. She defeated the trap and freed the Fairy Queen and past Crystal Keeper. Impressive for a beginning Crystal Keeper.

She has taken to her studies of energy direction nicely. But the Fairy Queen has told me much is still needed before she is completely ready. Her Cat Sorcerer, Brewford, has been overseeing some of her Crystal Keeper Training, as well as the elves. But it might not be fast enough to stop Balkazaar."

Castro stopped to gaze back into the far-seeing crystal. "There, another bee just entered through the Fairy Paths. I still can't follow it well enough to determine its reason for demise." Thump. His tail struck the stool he was balanced on. Thump. Castro jumped down and headed for his bookshelves. "I think I remember a book talking about the Fairy Paths and how they relate to energy transfer somewhere around here."

Rupert stepped forward and nodded upward. "I think it's on the second shelf master. The title if I remember was 'Energy Transfer and Fairy Paths: Guides and Reasons'. Isn't it written by the Master of Unicorns?"

"Yes Rupert. You remember your studies well. The Unicorns are still the main guides along the fairy paths. " He looked intently at the volume as it pulled itself out and lowered itself to the floor. Castro turned the pages slowly. "There. Yes, I was correct. Fairy Paths are a direct link to energies as well as paths to other Worlds of Fairy. Now, if I can only find why the bees are disappearing down them."

"Maybe the Unicorn Master can help?" suggested Rupert.

Castrotomas paused and looked up for a moment from the dusty volume. "Perhaps you're right. It might be time to ask others for help in this matter. And maybe to start directing this new promising Crystal Keeper to help us as well."

"Wonderful Master. Now that it is all settled, how about you have some food?" Rupert smiled at his master and Castro answered with a long-winded "Bah."

CHAPTER 1

The First Day of School

T hump. *Wanda, are you going to get up now?*

Fur rubbed against my arm after the initial pounce. I pushed Brewford off as he scampered towards the door of my bedroom. He looked back at me and then exited, tail raised. I started rubbing my eyes, the grass allergies from late summer driving them crazy as usual. Leaning back on my elbow, I tried to put off the inevitable. The first day of school loomed before me. All I had to do was get out of bed to start it. That was the problem.

If I just stayed in bed it might not happen, right? I could lay all day, reading that new series I found in the library last week about the girl who had secret powers and had to save the universe from an evil space-magician. Or I could get up, and just live it. After all, I had just become a Crystal Keeper, and danger was my game. My life was the plot in just about any fantasy book I could find in the library.

But the truth was I still didn't know where Balkazaar was, the Dark Sorcerer who was now free somewhere in the World of Fairy. I'm sure he wasn't happy with me for freeing the Crystal Keeper he'd caught last summer. I still didn't know how he had imprisoned Jordan, the old Crystal Keeper, so easily.

A lot had happened since I first followed that Crow-Fairy into the tree trunk. I'd discovered the World of Fairy was real, and now I was a caretaker to that World, or at least in my realm of the West. I'm what is called a Crystal Keeper. I, Wanda Stewart, was in charge of helping and saving the fairies when needed. Elves were helping to train me as well as promising to help with my homework. The Fairy Queen was helping me learn the different Fairy Realms. Our realm in the West was just one of many I was still learning about.

Then there were the other fairies, like the Brownies, Lavendora and Malik. They could enter the Real World in their animal forms, as a cat and a crow. Also, not to mention the fact that my own cat was a Sorcerer. Apparently, he is a Master Cat Sorcerer, which he all too frequently points out in my studies.

Anyway, I figured out that the mind trap had been linked to weaknesses. It kept bringing up all of Jordan's problems and not letting him look at the positive things. Poor Jordan got stuck in his own negative perspective of growing up. But I helped him come out of the mind trap by pointing out the positives, like going to college. It was the least I could do.

It was Balkazaar that had figured out Jordan's weakness. All I had to do was keep my own weakness a secret. As far as I knew, I didn't have any but one. Pretty simple.

I was still working on fixing my worst weakness. At least I knew what it was now, my confidence. I don't have much. But being a Crystal Keeper is helping some. I feel like I can solve a problem if I put my mind to it. Which brings me back to my current problem, getting out of bed and facing the first day of school. It wasn't going away.

Are you coming or not? Brewford's cat accented voice echoed in my mind. He added that stern cat-tone he always does when he's irritated.

"Yeah, Brew, I'm coming. Keep your whiskers on. You know, it's not always the easiest thing to get out of bed."

I know. Cats deplore it. But you have to get up so food can be given to you. Speaking of food, your mother is still in the glass box that sprays jets of water. **Mental shudder.** *I know how you humans allow water to be sprayed on you like that, but it just doesn't seem like a proper grooming.*

His head reappeared at the doorframe, ears peaked and twitching. He gave a quick shake to accent his thoughts. Then, he let out a loud "MEOW".

"All right, just hold on you ungrateful, fat cat."

Fat, who said fat? Nicely rounded and healthy I would think. He pointed his rump at me, tail up, and started to trek up the hall. I slid out onto the side of the bed, gave a nice stretch that started a yawn. Brewford turned and sat looking at me from the doorway of the bedroom. *I don't have all day.*

That is the one thing about helping the fairies now as a Keeper; I get back talk from my cat. I don't know who was worse now, Mom or him.

"Hey, sometimes we humans need a good stretch." I slid off the side of the bed and started towards the door. Brewford did a neat turn and almost tripped me as he rubbed against my legs. "Meow. Meow."

"Why all the fanfare Brew? You can just tell me you're hungry now."

We must keep up normal appearances. We can't let your mother or others know that things have changed. Being a Keeper has its responsibilities and secrets. "Meow. Meow." He led me down the hall, stopping at the opening to the kitchen.

"Laying it on a bit thick?" I whispered back at him.

Thick? How can I be thick? Is that another reference to my size?

"No, just that you are acting almost too cat-like." I reached for the cupboard where the cat food was stored. "Meow. Meow." I pulled the loop to open the can, and reached in the silverware drawer for a spoon. "Meow. Meow."

"Brewford sounds ready for his food," announced Mom as she came around the corner in her robe. She rubbed her wet hair with a towel as she stopped to see what I was doing. I feel like I'm always under the watchful eye.

"He is acting like he's starving again. You'd think he wouldn't since he's so FAT."

"MEOOOWW!"

I smiled down at him and he rubbed up against my legs one more time for effect. Scooping a few chunks of wet food, I plopped it into his bowl.

"How does it feel to be starting your first day of Middle School?" Mom switched to the other side of her head, shaking a bit to get her ears clear.

"I don't know, like starting last year. But I have a feeling it's going to be a lot different this year." I looked down at Brewford who had started to gobble with small grunting sounds.

She'll never know how different it's going to be. His mental voice held a timbre of humor.

I smiled at the thought. I didn't know how things were going to be at Middle School, but I knew they would be different. I was a Crystal Keeper now. I had secret powers, but I still wasn't sure how they worked even in the regular world. I still relied heavily on my fairy friends for help to enter and exit the Fairy World. I was getting better at it on my own. But I still needed help concentrating. The Fairy Queen had said I was coming along fine in my new powers and would be ready for new responsibilities soon. I didn't know what those were going to be either.

I opened another cupboard and got down the cereal. Looks like it was going to be a Cheerios day. I put the box onto the counter and went for the milk. The light of the refrigerator flickered as I opened the door. That had been happening a lot lately. Light bulbs popping; electrical items loosing power. Brewford said it was the energy output I had now as a Crystal Keeper. I could drain items of energy or overload it. I was supposed to get used to it. Well, I guess eventually I would.

I made my cereal and sat at the kitchen table. Mom threw the towel over a chair and started to make her own bowl. She looked at me with one of her far-away looks. "I remember my first day of Middle School. The school looked so big with so many kids. I felt like I was going to get swallowed up. It's so different than elementary school." She looked at me between bites of cereal. "Just remember, you won't get swallowed up, honey. It should be a piece of cake."

I nodded. Gotta humor your Mom, right? I wasn't really too worried about Middle School, except for running into Jessica. As long as Jessica Newark wasn't around, it would be ok. I'd had enough of her weirdo comments in Fifth Grade. I didn't want to run into more. Of course, that was elementary school. Maybe Middle School would be different.

I wonder if I'll be in James Murphy's class? Dang, I hadn't thought about him in a while. I could just imagine his green eyes staring at me during Math last year. But as long as I stayed away from Jessica, I figured I would be OK.

Of course, it didn't hurt to have a new tactic. I'm wearing black more. Black is a good color for me. It helps me feel like I'm invisible or at least less noticeable. I wonder if the fairies could actually teach me to be invisible? Being not noticeable was a good idea in dealing with Jessica and her cronies.

Not truly invisible. Brewford's mind speech buzzed through my head. *Though they could teach you how to blend in. So much so, that you'd seem invisible. It's what they do when in the physical world themselves. But you need to concentrate on getting to school. I'll miss taking my naps with you.*

"I will too Brew." I scratched under his chin and a purr sounded through the kitchen. "You're a cat, so how could you know about the first day of school?"

I've studied Cat Magics Wanda. There was a first day of school for me there. He had his especially huge Cat Smug Stare directed at me. I knew better than to fight that.

"Fine." I stopped scratching his chin. Brewford yowled his protest. "I have to start the First Day of School now, remember?" He did another cat yowl and got in a begging stance by the table. I wiped my mouth and got up from the table.

I think Mom was used to my one sided conversations with Brewford. She nodded. "Well, I guess it's time to pick out what to wear for the first day." Mom smiled and pointed to the direction of the hall closet. "Some of the outfits we got at the mall are hanging in the closet." We always put the special outfits there.

I'd chosen burgundy and black, my new power colors. The elves said it was a good idea to pick something that gave you strength. So, the color pattern was my new armor, and most of my new school clothes had the colors in them some how.

I got to the closet and picked out a plaid skirt and black turtleneck. Mom told me already you had to make a statement on the first day of school. Ok, whatever, because looking dressy was what Moms made you do on the first day, right? So, I picked a skirt that would go over well with teachers. Dressy is always good in that regard.

"Yeah, mom. I'll see you in a sec." I grabbed the outfit and scooted to my room. I saw a tabby tail enter as I pushed the door shut. "Heh, I could use some privacy."

You haven't before. Brewford looked up from his licking. His back leg posed in the air.

I gave him a weird look. "Nice look for you Brew. Really, things are different now that I know you can talk. I need privacy. Come on Brew, just for a moment."

Brewford's tail swished back and forth as he meowed by the door. I opened it, and he slid through. I tossed the clothes on quickly, and brushed my hair. Looking in the mirror, I did a quick inspection. The black turtleneck highlighted my crystal pendant. It gave a sparkle back at me as I picked it up. A voice started to buzz in my head as the crystal pendant warmed to my touch. My crystal fairy always talked to me when I held the crystal pendant. It was a symbol of being a Crystal Keeper. She was also a big helper, and always knew when to give the right advice.

The crystal fairy's voice tingled as she spoke in my head. *Ready for the first day? Remember you won't be alone.*

"Yeah," I thought back, "that's the one thing that I'll never forget. I'll never be alone again."

CHAPTER 2

First Meetings

Drexel Middle School loomed before me from the car window. I could imagine spires attached to the drab stark buildings. It looked more like boxes with windows than a school. Basically, it hadn't changed since my grandparents sent my parents there. It was almost prehistoric. Mom drove to the drop off spot and I opened the door.

"Remember to call me after you've walked home from the bus. I'm sorry I can't come get you, but now that you're in Middle School I can work longer hours."

"Yeah, I'll call you."

I closed the door. She started to drive away and looked back. I waved to keep her going. Parents could be so stifling. If only she knew what I'd fought and done to save the fairies. I think she'd trust me to be ok. But of course, if she knew, it could make it worse.

I grabbed my binder in the closed arm stance. The world seemed easier to face if you had your binder enfolded in front of you to face the world. I looked at the stream of kids entering the school and swam in. I glided next to Bethany Smith. I didn't know her very well, but at least it was someone to talk to. Better than the silent death of entering school by yourself, especially on the first day.

"Have a good summer?" I was hoping that she'd answer back. But she shook her head and moved a little faster. "Freak." Jessica Newark's voice rang in my ears as I looked behind me. Jessica moved closer with Marla Logan beside her.

Jessica continued. "I didn't know that it was time for the weird and strange to return from the jungle too." They broke up into an avalanche of laughter. I grabbed tighter onto my notebook and looked for a way out, away, anywhere.

My feet went into overdrive. I found a break in the masses of people and headed left. I still heard laughter behind me as I started looking at the room numbers. I tried to find my homeroom.

Ok, found Building F. Check. Now, looking at the door numbers I counted down. F-1, F-2, F-3. There, F-4. Luckily, it's the first thing I memorized off my schedule. I ducked in.

I sat down at the nearest desk hoping the safety of homeroom would keep anybody from noticing I was there. I got out my current fantasy novel, and didn't look up when other kids came in. I heard Jessica's voice come through the door. I glanced back to see her sit next to Carla Sanders. Great, Jessica and her clique were in my homeroom.

I turned back fast and kept my head down. My continued reading seemed the safest option. I wondered when I could get the fairies to help me become invisible.

"Nice crystal. I thought those were from the 80s? You like retro stuff?" I looked over at another girl sitting near me. She had short blonde hair, and was wearing a black t-shirt with jeans.

I nodded. "Yeah, I like crystals. Do you?" She nodded back and moved one desk closer to me. She set her binder on the desk in front of me. She had on slightly baggy clothes that looked just like they were from a thrift store. You know, the real retro-thing. She had blue eyes to go along with her short, straight blonde hair. A stream of freckles covered her nose, and there was a slight red tinge to her hair. Strawberry blonde I think it's called. Her favorite color seemed to be black, highlighted with cranberry.

She reached out her hand to me. "Hi, I'm Edina, but everyone calls me Eddie. I really like 80s music too. I think I was born in the wrong decade or something. You get the crystal at the Goodwill Store or something?"

I hadn't thought of an excuse of where I got my crystal yet. I didn't think people would notice it. It looked like normal jewelry. I held it for a moment under an impulse and a voice buzzed in my mind. *A store downtown specializes in crystals and crystal pendants. Say you got it there.*

"I got it at a boutique downtown."

"Breath of Avalon? Yeah, I like that store too."

The door opened and a man walked in with a suit. He had to be our teacher, Mr. Trenton. Everybody started shuffling to face forward, and the girl turned away.

He moved to the front of the class, deposited a briefcase on the desk, and motioned for us to be quiet.

"Welcome to the first day at Drexel. I'm Mr. Trenton. I'm your homeroom teacher and your Lit. Teacher for the semester. You'll have me the first two periods until you switch for your next class. This is a 6th grade homeroom class, so if you're in another grade; you're in the wrong room." He looked around to see if anyone was going to exit.

"Ok. Then, let's start attendance."

"Heh, what's your next class?" The reddish-blonde girl was following me down the hall. I stopped to let her catch up. I couldn't remember her name from talking before. Names are not my strong point, but I was too embarrassed to ask again.

"Math, I think. I have to look at my schedule."

She stopped next to me. "I memorized mine. It's easier than carrying it around. I got Science next. Then, Math. Then lunch. My favorite subject."

I laughed as she smiled back. "Yeah, me too."

"Then, maybe I'll see you later, ok? At lunch?" She looked expectant as her blue eyes focused on me.

"Yeah, sure, I'll see you later."

"Cool. Hope you survive Math."

"Me too."

I started down the hall towards the numbers labeling the Math wing and she started down the other way. Funny thing. This isn't what I expected the first day. I might have made a friend.

The cafeteria was a crowded mess. Wall to wall kids talked at volumes that could make elephants deaf. I was navigating the lunch line when Edina found me in front of the mashed potatoes. "How was Math?" She looked at me for an answer.

"I survived. You?" I answered while placing some applesauce on my tray. It looked the least dangerous.

"Yeah, Science turned out to be one giant project after another recited in order by our Science Teacher, Mr. Sanchez. The good thing is we only get pass or non-pass grades. It's this new way of teaching he's trying on us. Makes me feel like a guinea pig. Hmmm. Cinnamon Crumb Cake."

We stopped and both dove into our food score. After sliding through the lunch check out, we headed for a table. Laughter stopped us. I saw Jessica pointing with her gang of cronies, Morgan and Carla on either side. Jessica swept up to us before we had a chance to escape.

"Looks like the weird-one has found an escort. Nice pair, I think." Giggles followed Jessica's statement.

I was frozen like a deer in headlights. Edina answered for us both. "Get lost, trendy losers." She tried to swing away another direction, but got blocked by the trio.

"Not so fast weirdo. Wanda picked a good match up for a friend. I didn't know she could make a friend, after being such a loser at gymnastics class." More laughter followed.

"Do you know this idiot?" said Edina motioning towards Jessica.

"Back in elementary school," I said rolling my eyes a bit following her lead. We were like two players at charades already. I could get her drift that fast.

"Well, you're with me now. Let's go hang out with a better crowd. This is definitely not elementary school." She bumped trays to get me moving another direction She added over her shoulder, "See ya. And wouldn't want to be ya."

We escaped to the far side of the cafeteria among some others of similarly dressed in black. I think I'd found my clique. Double score for the first day.

As we walked up, one girl motioned to Eddie. "Got a place open here Eddie. Who's your new friend?" We all slid down the bench as several pairs of eyes all turned to us.

"This is Wanda." Edina waved to everyone around the table. "This is the gang of weirdoes." They all laughed back.

I laughed too. "Guess I'll fit right in."

One of the girls next to me swung around, her black hair covering one side of her face. "So Wanda, who do you like more, Edward or Jacob?"

"What? I don't know which is who yet. Is one of them sitting across from us?"

"No," the girl shook her head. "From the book *Twilight*, which do you like more, the vampire Edward or the werewolf Jacob?"

"Oh, I haven't read it yet. But I've got to get it on my list." There I think that covered it. I'd only heard of the book in

Fifth Grade, but my mom wouldn't let me read it yet. I was too embarrassed to tell them though.

Eddie gave me a look then answered, "You know Pam, not everyone has read it yet. My mom still says I can't read the series until I'm like 13."

Wow, thanks Eddie. She totally came to my rescue. But Pam wouldn't let up. She looked right at me and said, "But you must have seen the movie, right?"

"Well, not yet. I've been busy this summer, and I haven't seen any of the Twilight movies." I figured if fairies were real, maybe I shouldn't be reading about vampires quite yet. They could be coming out of the woodwork next.

Pam flipped the hair out of her eyes again. Her green eyes looked at me very serious. "I am definitely in Club Edward." She smiled a grin like it was the biggest secret in the world.

"I'm definitely Club Jacob. Werewolves are so much cooler," answered a girl across from us.

"Clare, you would." Pam turned to her and continued. "You always side on anything having to do with dogs in general."

"That's because puppies are so cute. But I do have my Native American heritage." She smiled with big brown eyes outlined in heavy dark liner and mascara.

The bell rang, and I realized I had barely gotten down my food.

"I hate it when lunch goes by too fast," I said as I stood up with my tray.

"Don't we all?" chimed in Eddie as we walked together to dump our leftovers in the trash. "I'll see you maybe after school?"

I nodded.

"Meet me at the front, kay? I know of a cool place we can hang out at after school." Eddie waved and turned to catch up to walk with Pam. I was left on my own to face my next two classes, PE and Social Studies. I didn't know which I was dreading the most.

It wasn't hard to spot Eddie after school. Not that many people have strawberry blonde hair, or dress in black to accent the strangeness. I walked up not sure if that friendly person was going to continue talking to me like at lunch. This whole friends business was not my usual thing. My closest friend had been Michelle. We'd been buds since Kindergarten, and then she moved away last summer. Sometimes I'd email her, but it wasn't the same as talking in real time. The fairies kept me from being totally lonely, but sometimes a Crystal Keeper needs other friends, human friends.

"So how was the afternoon? You survive PE?" She was still smiling. That's always a good sign.

"Yeah, we mostly just sat around and talked. PE is pretty boring apparently until we start to dress out. That is supposed to be starting next week. Social studies was scary. This teacher Mrs. Wilkinson wants to dump tons of work on us. She's talking about weekly essays about everything in American History."

"Typical first day. Scare us into being good and doing our homework everyday."

I blinked. I'd always done my homework. But I think it was a cue to make a witty come back. So I answered, "Spoken like a true rebel."

Edina shrugged. "School is one of those things that just has to be. Why be upset by it? There are worst things. Starvation, homelessness, pollution..."

"And who do we have here. The Goth twins. Isn't that just special." Jessica walked up with Morgan behind her. "I should have known you'd be hanging out after school. Nobody else to play with, boo hoo." Jessica's nasal tone emphasized the boo hoo and she pretended to rub her cheek.

"You know, what is your problem?" Edina's tone rose sharply. "You don't have to follow us around, unless you can't fit in with the popular crowd already. They disown you already trendy girl?"

Edina gave an outlandish laugh and grabbed my arm pulling me away from them both. Jessica's mouth flapped like a surprised guppy. I don't think anyone had said that to her in elementary school. I was glad this was Middle School now.

People seemed to stare at us as we walked by. I was wearing black and burgundy plaid, and she wore black and cranberry. It was like we had the same weird fashion sense. And Edina just held her head proudly. Like she knew it was cool to dress this way. I'd never been in fashion before.

"So, where is this cool place?" I said after we'd gotten away and out of the school grounds. If I had learned anything this summer, it would be that nothing is how it seems.

"There's just a place I like to go not too far from the school. It's in a park nearby. You'll like it. It's a place to just chill."

"I guess that's why it's so cool."

She gave me an odd look. "Yeah, ha-ha. Really, what school did you go to last year?"

"Livingston Elementary."

"Wow, I went to Johnson. Your school is way across town from here. I live over where they're building the new mall. We can take the bus to that shop I was telling you about sometime later maybe."

"That would be cool." I nodded my head. Maybe this friend thing wasn't so hard after all. It could ruin my loner image though.

"We're almost there now," Eddie said as she motioned in front of us.

We were coming around a corner of a busy street, and then I could see the park. It was at least a block long, full of trees, with a hill in its center. On top of the hill was a large tree. "Here we are." Eddie pointed to the tree. "I'll race you."

Do you know how hard it is to race holding your binder and your backpack full of books? Well, you have to get that right rhythm, or you'll fall over. I think Eddie had it mastered because she won the race. She was waiting for me as I came panting up the hill. She was standing next to a tree, and in the branches above was a black squirrel.

We're glad you have arrived safely. Welcome to Glenford Faery Hill, Wanda.

The squirrel gave me a wink. Eddie pulled a crystal from underneath her shirt and smiled.

CHAPTER 3

Adventures in Friendship

J ust when I thought all the surprises of the first day of school were over, here was another Crystal Keeper standing right in front of me.

"We Keepers have to stick together, right Broc?" said Eddie as she nodded at the squirrel. It chatted back a chit, chit, but in my mind I heard, *Yes, Edina, Keepers need to help each other.*

"I can't believe you're a Keeper too?" There was some hint of surprise still in my voice as I looked back at her. After all, I was still getting used to Middle School and maybe having a new friend. For her to be a Keeper was too good to be true.

She smiled back. "What did you expect? Besides Jordan was getting too old. I figured he'd have a replacement soon. So how's your training going?"

Eddie and the squirrel looked at me as if I was an equal. Just hey, what's up in your neck of the forest? It was something I hadn't felt before. I didn't want to blow it. So I tried to look at ease as Eddie looked at me.

"Pretty well. The Fairy Queen mentioned I would need some further instruction since I'd done a lot of the basics of Keeper Magic during the summer." Wait a sec. I gave Eddie a steady look. "Do you know something about my training that I don't?" I could smell a set-up, especially if the Fairy Queen was in on it. The one thing about fairies, they didn't do anything by chance.

Eddie gave me a measured look. "I've been at this for a few years now. Jordan helped me. I'm going to return the favor. Besides, with Balkazaar running around, we need all of the Crystal Keepers up and running at top speed. I'm going to show you some of the ropes."

"So you're my new tutor?" I asked.

Eddie nodded. I continued feeling incredibly at ease. "I thought it was going to be another elf."

Eddie laughed and the squirrel rolled onto it's back, feet waving in the air.

Elves just think they know everything. The squirrel kept rolling around with its chit, chit snicker.

"Sometimes it takes another Keeper to explain what it's really like to help the fairies." Eddie shrugged her shoulders. A Crystal Keeper needs training from another Keeper eventually. That would be me." She pointed to herself ending with a bow. Then, she gestured towards the tree. It was an Oak, majestic and shady up on the hill. It seemed very inviting on a hot end-of-August day. But I knew what to do. I took a deep breath, held my crystal, and stepped into the trunk. I felt like a pro now since I've had enough practice entering through my fairy tree.

My eyes had to adjust to the dim light of the crystals that lined the walls. This was similar to the tunnel entrance to my World of Fairy, but there were yellow quartz crystals lining the walls to light our way. It looked like the color of the street lamps that came on at night.

"This way. I have someone you need to meet." I followed Eddie down the corridor and stumbled slightly around a corner. I felt a bump from behind. A brownie fairy was right next to me. He gave me a bit of a nudge as I tried to get better footing. His hair was black-brown and his small nose was like a stub. He had beady black eyes that he turned at me as we walked together. I realized this was squirrel boy I'd met earlier in his other form.

As I kept walking, I felt something sharp under my foot. "Give me a second, 'kay? A stone or something must' a got stuck in my shoe when I stumbled."

He nodded. "When you are ready then." I took my shoe off and noticed a small yellow crystal at the bottom. "Strange how a crystal wormed it's way into my shoe."

"Sometimes you pick up things you may need later in the World of Fairy," said squirrel boy as he wiggled his nose. "It is always wise to hold onto things that you might find here. You may need them later." He sounded very cryptic as I slowly looked at the crystal. It was a small shard, most likely broken from the walls. It had a sulphur color, but was very clear.

"It couldn't hurt to hold on to it, I guess." I put it in my pocket, and he gestured down the corridor. I couldn't see where Eddie had gone. I followed the rest of the corridor, through some turns small and large, that finally led to a wooden door. This was similar to other doors I'd seen in the World of Fairy. And yes, this one had no knobs or openings of any kind.

"Hmm, I wonder if all doors in the Fairy World work the same." I looked to squirrel boy, or what was it, Broc? He just continued to look at me.

"Any suggestions?" I tried to hide my nerves by sounding earnest.

"You are the Keeper. I follow you." He rubbed his nose and just kept looking at me with those beady eyes. Right. Definitely no help there. I was starting to feel like problem solving was a Keeper's middle name.

I knocked on the door. Nothing happened. I pushed on it. Nothing. I blew on it. Nothing! This seems awfully familiar. I held my crystal to see if the fairy within had a suggestion.

Luckily, the voice bubbled into my mind immediately. *Every entrance to Faery has a door to pass. The secret is within you to find it.*

Well, I should have known better. Nothing in the World of Fairies is easy. Challenges seem to spur you into everything here.

Wait, maybe that was it? If this was a challenge, I had something inside me to solve it. The last time this happened, I wished for it to open. Could it be that simple again?

"I wish for this door to allow me to enter the World of Fairy."

The door vaporized, like it was an illusion, though I'd been banging and pushing it before. I walked through into a large crystal chamber studded with deep purple amethysts. A great throne, made of amethysts, was positioned on a dais in the center of the chamber. It started to turn towards me. A seated figure, about half my height, sat in the chair. I saw Eddie standing at the base of the dais, off in the shadows. At this point, I started to worry if this was a trap. I'd run into them before.

"Well done in opening the door. Many don't make use of their prior experiences and don't make it into the inner chamber of Glifford Faery Glen. I'm Alira, Queen Wood Sprite of the Great Oak Council. I have a problem to address with you."

I haven't even gotten a chance to start on my first day of homework, and already there's a new problem to deal with. I looked at Eddie. She just stayed in the shadows looking at the creature on the throne.

I noticed that the wood sprite queen was all green skinned, with flowing green material for a dress. The dress was shaped like leaves draping her body. Her long, flowing green hair and yellow diamond eyes bored a hole through my mind as she looked at me. I couldn't look away.

"All right, you've got my attention. Your Keeper has brought me here. What is it that you need?" I mean, that's what a Crystal Keeper is supposed to say, right? I was hoping I sounded like a heroine out of one of my favorite books. Sometimes reading a lot of fantasy novels came in handy as a Keeper.

"There is a problem among the Kingdoms of Fairy. And we need the minds of all Crystal Keepers to try to solve it. It involves bees."

"Bees?" I hate bees. I got stung once when I was 5. It swelled up and my mom had to take me to the hospital. I'd been warned to stay away from them. "What about bees?" I almost felt like not asking. However, I'd found out the direct approach is the best way to go with fairies.

Queen Alira sighed and said, "They are dying. The way of the wood has been disrupted and somehow the bees are affected. They are our close allies in fostering trees and other plant life. Without bees, much of our forests and plants would not continue on."

"Not to mention that honey is an excellent byproduct." Eddie chimed in with a big grin.

Queen Alira nodded. "It is a gift from the bees to all and again the weight of their function in forest and glen. It is a harsh problem. Whole hives have been found dead or abandoned. We know not how this is possible, and we look to you, the Keepers, for assistance in this grave matter. We believe they might be disappearing through the ley line doorways." She lowered her head and focused her attention squarely to my eyes. "It is most grave." The wood sprite looked towards Edina.

Eddie cleared her throat. "So, I figure, we've got to do some research on why the bees might be dying, in a Keeper sense. That's why I guessed we could head to the crystal store downtown. Sometimes the answers have been hidden in myths and legends. The knowledge of past Keepers got turned into stories and stuff. You ready to check it out?"

Eddie jumped down off the dais and started to head down the corridor.

"What about homework?" I tried to hide the fact it sounded more like a nervous yelp. If my grades went down from being a Keeper, grounded would be my past time.

"Don't worry. There are some top elves that help with homework. Maybe I'll introduce you to the elf that helps me with mine. He's great at doing Algebra."

That did make me feel a bit better. The elves had promised to help me with homework this year. I'd forgotten in my panic. Maybe Algebra won't be so scary after all.

From that I took a cue to bow slightly to the Queen, and headed down the corridor after Eddie. This year was not going to be anywhere close to what I thought it was going to be.

It wasn't far to the bus stop from the park. It was going to be at least 10 minutes until the bus arrived. It was a well-traveled route with other kids like us all hanging out waiting for the bus. Eddie and I tried to get out of the main crowd, especially since I didn't want to run into anybody from my old school. What would Eddie say to them? Hey, this is my new buddy that is into crystals like me. And by the way, have you seen fairies? I don't think the rest of the world was ready for fairies yet. At least not real ones.

Getting out of the crowd worked at least. We headed over to a bus stop that didn't include my route home. How was I going to get home? Ok, don't panic. You're on a Crystal Keeper Quest. Finding out about how to help the fairies by going to a crystal store is a logical place to start. But how do I explain it to Mom? Wait. I could call her. "Eddie, is there a phone booth or something near the store?" I tried to not sound too worried.

I had a tendency to worry too much and show it. Sometimes it drove me a little crazy.

Eddie stopped looking down the road for the bus. "You can use my cell phone to call home if you want." She dug in her backpack. "You need it now?" She looked up at me from her stance of balancing her backpack on her foot.

"No, maybe it would be better to call her once I'm there. It's downtown right? I used to go before with my friend, Michelle, on Saturdays. It's always better to let my mom know I'm ok, and where I am. She likes that. But it's hard when I have to use payphones. They're hard to find now."

"You can't get a cell phone?"

"Too expensive. Mom doesn't have one herself right now. The divorce is making it hard to make ends meet, she says."

"Sorry Wanda. I remember when my parents got divorced. It was hard not having my mom around, but at least the fighting stopped."

"You live with your Dad?

"Yeah, my mom went into the Peace Corps. She said she needed to find herself, and left not too long after my 9ᵗʰ birthday." She picked up her backpack and let it hang on her shoulder. "If it hadn't been for the fairies, I don't think I'd gotten through it all. My dad is ok, but he's not around a lot. But at least the fairies are there for me."

"Yeah, they have made me feel less lonely since Michelle moved."

The sound of the bus pulling up changed the conversation into a scurry for our backpacks. We filed into line and found two seats together. We balanced backpacks on the floor and were able to steady ourselves as the bus lurched ahead.

"So, what did you think of Mr. Trenton's class? I had to keep from falling asleep. I hate reading class." Eddie leaned forward with her backpack between her legs and one arm under her chin.

I pushed back my glasses. "I don't know. I like reading since it puts me in another world. I hate having to be told what to read. Assigned reading sucks."

Eddie leaned back in her seat and sighed. "It would be nice to read what I'd like to. I think I'd like reading more that way. It was pretty boring, beginning of school stuff today. 'Here's your books. Read the intro to your Literature book and we'll talk about it tomorrow.' "

I nodded as the bus jostled over a bump. I grabbed onto the yellow pole next to the seat. "I really like reading though. So Lit. Class is going to be fun, I hope."

"I don't know how you can like reading all those books? Give me a good anime, and I'm happy. Do you like anime?"

"I think I've seen some of the books at the library. But I usually head right to the Fantasy Sci-Fi section."

"You'll like the books at the crystal store. A lot of them are fantasy books. Plus, there's a lot on fairies. It's like a special place to do research as a Crystal Keeper."

"Really, like better than the library?"

"Much better." Eddie leaned closer from her backpack and whispered in my ear. "It's specialized. The owner used to be a Crystal Keeper." I gave Eddie the 'really?' look. I remembered the things the Fairy Queen had said to Jordan in the mind-trap maze. *Many ex-Keepers go out into the world to help the fairies.* How many ex-Keepers were out there?

The bus had turned the corner onto the main street downtown. "Time to get off", Eddie announced as she pushed the little bar that signaled the driver to stop. "We're just a few blocks away from the shop taking this line. But at least it's a nice walk. We even go past a McD's. Want to stop for a cup of something?"

I shook my head. "I don't drink soda."

"Neither do I. But they have good smoothies. Jamba Juice has the best smoothies, but they are back the other way. Sure you don't want to get something?"

I nodded again. I didn't want to say I didn't have any spare cash. I had bus pass money, but that was all in the budget. Snacks were not an option unless I was at home. But I couldn't tell Eddie. What would she think? I couldn't even get a smoothie if I wanted one.

But the bus stopped my thoughts as we started to roll to a stand still. We crowded the aisle with the other people trying to get off. A little girl pulling on her mom's hand pointed at me. "Hey, there's a people in her sparkly. Look, pretty sparkly people." Her mom pulled her back. I grabbed my crystal pendant and slipped it under my shirt.

We got off the bus and Eddie looked back to make sure we had some distance from the other passengers. "Kids can see the fairy in the pendant." She was speaking in the 'we've got secrets' tone. "Sometimes I hide mine, but with retro clothing, crystals are fashionable. It's a great way to hide the fairy crystal pendant in the open. But the store might have other ways you can wear it or you could carry it in a pouch."

We adjusted backpacks as we sped into a walk. Eddie could set a quick pace. I had the odd thought that she must really work out. Or had I just been hanging out with my cat too much and was used to his pace. Real kid pace was a lot faster.

We past the McD's and a cookie store that looked tempting. This part of downtown was a snack trap. My stomach did a rumble as if to protest we weren't stopping. However, Crystal Keeper business was important business. Eddie didn't slow until we got to the end of the downtown outdoor mall. We went up behind some of the main storefronts, and in the back part of a shopping court. A sign painted with rainbows and pastels spelled out "Breath of Avalon". I took a breath and stepped through the doorway. What could happen in a crystal store, right?

CHAPTER 4

The Crystal Store

Here we were. At least it was easy stepping through the door. The door chimes reminded me of the Fairy Queen's lyrical voice.

I took a look around the store. There was a musty smell of roses as I walked back along the shelves. There were displays of crystals, of every shape and size. Different figurines of fairies were shown on a table near the front of the store. The nooks and crannies of the place were stuffed full of candles, crystals, and books. Eddie headed to the small section of books near the back.

I followed her, like some sort of sidekick. After turning an aisle corner, I noticed a giant grey tabby sitting on a couch by the books. A table nearby was strewn with more books. The cat took a moment from it's grooming to look at me, and continued. I guess I passed inspection.

There was another tinkle of bells, and beads that were hiding an opening from the back parted wide. A woman entered at a brisk pace. She noticed us in the book nook, and waved for us to continue. "If you see anything you're interested in, please give a shout." She squinted a bit. "Oh, hey there Eddie. I see you brought a friend this time."

Eddie motioned at me and answered, "Her name is Wanda. I wanted to bring her in to show her the place."

"Well, let me know if you have any questions," said the woman. She began to sit at a stool behind the desk near the front. "Most people come in with questions." She looked directly at me, as if she could read my mind. Green eyes locked me in her glance. I had to shake my head a bit to get my thoughts straight.

"Yeah, I guess I have one. It's about ley lines. Do you know anything about them?"

She took a moment to put on some glasses she had sitting on the desk and walked over to the bookshelves. "I think there is a section on Ley Lines and Stone Circles. They work together you know." She started to run her finger along the spines of books. "Yes, here are some." She scanned the shelves pointing to one book after another. "Were you interested in a particular place? Great Britain, perhaps? Or how about this book on Ireland?"

"Both would work, I think." I shrugged. "I'm not sure which I need really."

"Well, look them over, and let me know if I can help you further."

She let her glasses fall and hang by a crystal wrapped cord. I noticed a sparkle around her neck, and saw a pendant, like my own. It was exactly like the one I was wearing, except the leather cord was much more worn. She looked at me with a knowing look and winked. "Keepers need to stick together Wanda."

Before I could answer, she returned to her desk and I turned to see Edina looking at me. "What did you expect? You haven't been at this too long. Keepers help out other Keepers. Mrs. Lawrence used to be a Keeper 20 years ago. Kinda cool, right? The fairies referred me to her shop when I first started. Hey, you look like you've seen a ghost."

I guess I looked shocked. I tried to relax a bit. "No, it's just that I thought I was the only one."

"Well, isn't it good to know you're not?" Edina started to pick out a book that Mrs. Lawrence pointed out to me. "I think we're going to need all the help we can get. Grab a book. Let's see what we can find before dinner."

Picking a book that looked interesting, The Ley Lines of Ireland, I dove into a description on how ley lines worked and guided energy through the Irish countryside. The legends described about how the ley lines were the fairy paths of old. They are how energy travels through the Earth, connecting areas of power. It described on page 23:

"Ley lines are the traveling paths that energy takes through the ground. Following them leads to power centers on the planet. Legends date back to times when fairies used them as ways into their world or even to travel from place to place. The stone circles of Ireland are said to be built at the nodes of these lines."

"I think I found something. Listen to this Eddie." I read aloud what I had found.

Eddie shook her head and commented, "It's a start, but it still doesn't tell us why the bees are dying. It tells us how they might be traveling from place to place."

"Do you think the bees might be disappearing into these power nodes? The book says the intersections of the ley lines can be very powerful." I paused for a moment. Sometimes watching enough Star Trek episodes can inspire a person with ideas. "I mean, they might just disappear and reappear somewhere else, kinda like a vortex or something. Maybe even like a black hole? Do you know how to travel on the ley lines?"

Eddie gave me a shrug. "From what I've explored, you need a guide for the ley lines. What does it say in the book?"

I looked in the index for traveling along ley lines and found nothing.

"What about asking Mrs. Lawrence?" suggested Eddie.

As if thinking of her made her magically appear, Mrs. Lawrence poked her head into the book nook. "How is the search going?"

"Do you know anything about traveling on ley lines?" I asked.

She took a moment to look down, and turned her glasses in her fingertips. "Rarely did I have to travel the ley lines as a Keeper. But when I did, I had a guide."

"See, I told you." Eddie had an 'I told you so' look to match. "I thought you'd know how to help us. How do you find the guides?"

"The guides find you Edina," Mrs. Lawrence continued to twirl her glasses. "And they usually appear when they are needed the most."

"I hate waiting." Eddie looked at her watch. "It's just about dinner time. We should be heading back."

I noticed the sunlight fading through the front window of the store. "Yeah, if I'm late getting home the first day, I'll be totally busted.

Eddie closed her book. "Luckily, there isn't much homework the first day of school."

"You lucked out then. I've got a whole page to write about what I think Social Studies is tonight."

Eddie gave me a sympathetic look. "You got Mrs. Wilkinson?" I nodded as Eddie continued. "She's tough I hear. Watch out for her pop quizzes, especially the ones on Fridays."

"Who told you that?" I asked with wonder.

"The elves," answered Eddie. "They know all the tricks for getting through school."

"Was the first day of school today?" Mrs. Lawrence chimed in. "What grade are you in now Eddie?" She smiled with a look of memories edging her thoughts.

"Middle school, sixth grade." Eddie picked up her backpack and I followed suit.

I pushed up my glasses again. I was thinking of the long bus ride back home. New friends were fabulous, but I didn't want to get grounded on my first day back to the old grind.

"Well, we better be off. We'll come back if we need more info." Eddie grabbed my hand. "Come on Wanda. We can still catch the 5:20 bus."

Mrs. Lawrence gave a little wave as we scooted through the door. The tinkling bell echoed behind as we did a dash to the bus stop.

And the book said that the ley lines were the fairy paths? Brewford was sitting looking at me with his serious cat look. *The doorways are usually difficult to enter. Keepers need guides and sorcerers...* He gave a twitch to his whiskers. *However, sorcerers would have no trouble guiding energy through the doorways. They feed on the energy of the ley lines and the gathered energy at the power sources. This could be dire indeed.*

"You sound like the Queen Tree Sprite, Brew."

Queen Tree Sprite?

"Yeah Brew. She's the one that told me all about the bees and stuff."

He held his head down, and took a moment to sort it out like I do. After the pause he added, *She is right about the seriousness of the situation. Bees are great helpers to the Fairies. They are the main messengers of the Fairy World and the steeds to the Pillywiggin fairies, a type of flower fairy. There are many factors involved I fear. This could be a very dangerous situation if the Queen of the Oak Council is involved.*

"Oak Council? Bees? What's so important? And besides, I thought they just pollinated the flowers."

Pollination is really important. But they carry the messages from flower to flower, from one flower fairy to another. They are also the messengers to the forest and glen. And the Oak Council helps govern the many Kingdoms of Fairy. Without the Bees, the fairies would be unlikely to communicate.

I shook my head. "And the Unicorns are messengers too?"

Don't sound surprised Wanda. After all, being a Keeper the last few months has made your energies very attuned to the Fairy World. Unicorns are the guardian messengers. They carry messages between the Fairy Realms. I'm amazed a unicorn hasn't shown up yet with some serious issue from some other Fairy Realm.

"Unicorns, dead bees, ley lines...."I shook my head and grabbed my temples. "It's been a busy day."

Yet, most productive. Brewford did a 360-degree turn inspection of where to sleep on my bed. *I suggest we get some sleep. You have school tomorrow, and the Fairy World to save, again. You need your rest.*

"You don't have to tell me that twice." I turned over and grabbed my pillow. I adjusted it to my favorite shape, bending my arm beneath it. "At least, I'm not alone."

I felt Brewford lean against my foot, and that was the last thing I remembered until morning.

CHAPTER 5

School Vs. Keeper

"**A**nd the Western States stretch from California to Washington." Mrs. Wilkinson's voice droned on about the other states of the West, leading into the South Western states. I was half listening, with the rest of my thoughts on ley lines and bees. It had already been a couple of days, and still Queen Alira was reporting more dead bees at the doorways to the ley line paths. Nothing else had changed, except I was having trouble concentrating in Social Studies.

"Wanda...again, tell me the states that are considered the Four Corners states?"

I was bumped out of my contemplation of the situation by Mrs. Wilkinson's voice pounding for an answer. "Ah…"

Not the best way to start. I tried again. "Could you repeat the question?"

"What are the Four Corners states?" She looked down at me and was standing in front of my desk. "And if you weren't listening, here's a clue. They were in the region I was just discussing."

I hate it when teachers were tricky if not mean, even if I hadn't been listening. Sometimes a little respect is helpful in keeping a person's attention. But then, that thought wasn't going to get me out of this situation. The right answer would. What was she saying, the Western States, South Western… wait.

"The Four Corners States are Colorado, Arizona, New Mexico and Utah."

"Correct. I hope you remember that for the quiz this Friday on US Regions and Geography." There was a collective groan from the class. Well, at least I knew I wasn't the only one regretting the first quiz of the year. I slumped a little down in my seat, trying to remember the southwestern states. My notes started to look like a jumble of squiggles as I tried to write down the information. Maybe I'd have to look through the first two chapters again. The problem was when? I had to go meet Edina after school today to head to the crystal store. There had to be something about the ley lines we had missed.

Later on the bus heading for "Breath of Avalon", I was full of questions. It was like a dam had broken in my mind, and all I could think about was the ley lines and how the bees were dying. I was trying to look over my notes from Social Studies, but Edina kept interrupting me

"You said your Cat Guardian mentioned that only another sorcerer could pull that much power to draw the bees?" I guess Eddie was full of questions too.

"Cat Guardian? I thought he was just my cat."

"Oh, cats are guardians of children. So are dogs. Really depends on what the person likes. But cats can direct more energy and tend to be sorcerers too. Dogs are more for the warrior type of Keeper."

"There are different types of Keepers?", I said with questions flooding my voice.

"Boy Wanda, where have you been all summer?"

"Studying with the Elves all the new spells and powers I need to be a good Keeper."

"Oh, that explains a lot. You're being trained to be a Sorcerer Keeper. I'm a Warrior Keeper. No wonder they paired us up. A warrior and sorcerer Keeper make a great team. " Eddie held out her hand. "I believe it makes us partners in Keeper adventures."

I held out my hand too. "Partners."

As we shook hands, Eddie said, "You know, we could come up with a secret handshake or something. You know, only for us Keepers."

I nodded. "Yeah, just for the two of us or something. Like our own secret club."

"Which being a Keeper in itself is like it's own secret club. But back to Keeper business. We're almost to the store. And I've been wondering, how do you think the bees are involved?"

I shrugged. "Ley lines draw the power. The bees are drawn to it I imagine. So..."

"Could there be something else?" Eddie insisted.

"I don't know." I paused to take a moment. I tried to think of where we could find more info. "Maybe we could find it in the ley lines book at the store or we could ask Mrs. Lawrence." I suddenly remembered my homework for the night. Hate it when that creeps in. "I can't stay long. I've got to study some for this quiz on Friday. I want to try to keep up my "A" average, and I think Middle School is so much harder than 5th grade."

"You're telling me. I've got 35 problems in Algebra and Gelvin, my elf tutor, can't come until tomorrow. You know anything about Algebra?"

I shook my head. "My mom is pretty good though. She helps me most the time."

"At least you have a mom. Mine writes to me from Zimbabwe, but it's not the same as her being here. But hey, I've got the fairies, right?"

I gave Edina a nod. "Yeah, we've got the fairies."

The bus came to a halt. I started shoving my notebook away trying to hide my feeling of regret. I didn't know Eddie missed her mom so much. I felt totally bad. At least I did have my mom, even if she always gave me a bad time about where I was and if I didn't do my homework.

"Come on, I'll race you to the shop." She ducked around some teenagers stepping down from the bus and sprinted from the door. I tried to get by, but got stuck behind. She had a good lead by the time we went by McD's. She was waiting by the door, out of breath, but with a big smile on her flushed face.

"I might try out for track later this year. Think I'll get in?"

I laughed. Maybe having a friend was knowing the right thing to say and knowing when not to say a thing. I didn't even need a moment.

"Yeah, you sure beat me."

The tinkling of the bell announced our entrance, and Mrs. Lawrence came over to us from the front desk. "You girls still searching for Ley Line information?"

"Sure, " said Eddie easing her backpack onto a chair in the book nook. "What do ya' got?"

Mrs. Lawrence went back to her front desk, picked up a rather thin book, and brought it back to us. She handed it over to Eddie, and she waved me over to look at the cover. "The Secrets of the Green Man: A Discovery of Ley Lines and Other Mysteries of Ireland."

"Wow! This might have the answer!" I squeaked sounding too much like a first grader to recover.

Edina saved me from total kid embarrassment. "Thanks Mrs. L. This should tell us something."

We plopped down on the leather couch and opened the book slowly. The pages were beautiful, with lots of pictures of Celtic Knot work that I'd seen in some of the other books. Then we turned to the page with the Green Man.

It was a beautiful picture of intertwining leaves that formed a man smiling back. His face was made of leaves while his body was knotted with vines, twigs, and leaves. He stood in a grove of Oak trees. Behind him were creatures of the forest, rabbits, foxes, birds, squirrels, and an elk.

"Wow. The artwork is amazing! It's better than some of my graphic novels." Eddie looked the picture up and down. "Do you see some bees in the background of the picture? They are swarming around the plants and than looking like they disappear into the bushes."

I squinted to get a closer look. It did look like yellowish winged creatures were disappearing among the flowers on one side. "What is the Green Man anyway?"

Eddie pointed to the caption. Along the bottom of the page it said:

"The Green Man is an ancient legend that dates back to well before the Romans conquered the British Isles. He is a mythical spirit in charge of the well-being of the forest and its creatures. The Green Man is said to imbue the energy of the forest and to watch the well-being of all things.

He is often portrayed as a living man made up of green vines and leaves. Most often, he can be found carved into medieval church pillars and buildings for protection. His image can be found in different parts of Ireland, Wales and England."

"Oh yes, the Green Man. He is a real character indeed." Mrs. Wilkinson leaned over my shoulder as I turned to hear.

"You act like he's not imaginary or something," said Eddie as she turned the page to look at the next picture. It showed the Green Man in the forest, this time in the fall. Leaves were brown, orange, and red with the wind blowing a whirl of twigs around him.

"But he is real." Mrs. Wilkinson looked at us slowly. "Many true things have been lost into the myths. He has become hidden because the world has lost its respect for him. As soon as people wish to find him again, he will reappear."

"So do you think he can help? Maybe he'd know why the bees are disappearing?"

I pushed back my glasses as I gave myself a moment. "I mean, if he's in charge of all living things, maybe he knows what is happening to the bees."

"It may be so. But he is not easy to find. I only know of him when he found me. It was back when I needed help as a Keeper. It may be…" she stopped and pointed at me. "He may find you."

She smiled and walked away before I could ask the question I was thinking. How would he find me? But then I realized what time it was. Time to study. Shouldn't let my grades slip even if I was trying to save the Fairy World, again. I was hoping Eddie would understand.

"I think I'm going to go home. I need to study or I'm totally going to fail the quiz on Friday."

Eddie gave me a long look, then answered. "Ok, I'll stay here. If I find anything, how about I give you a call."

Good. That wasn't so bad. Sometimes this friend thing makes me nervous. I smiled at the thought of talking to someone on the phone again. I hadn't talked to a friend since Michelle moved away. "Yeah, I'd like that. Let me know what you find anyway. I'll need a break from geography facts."

I picked up my backpack and headed towards the door. Mrs. Wilkinson gave me a wave as the tinkling bells announced my exit.

Later at home lying in bed, I was thought-talking what I found out with Brewford.

"So, that's what we found so far." I pulled the covers up and lay back against my pillow. "You think the Green Man can help?"

It couldn't hurt to ask for help when it is needed Wanda. He adjusted himself on the bed. His favorite sleeping position was always with his leg under his chin. It looked awkward, but it made him a tabby cat ball, with big green eyes. *After all, you remembered to ask me for help with the healing spring water hunt.* He lifted his head and blinked. *Sometimes wisdom is knowing when to call for help.*

I took a moment. Yeah, help would be good right now. But how was I going to get a hold of the Green Man? It's not like the fairies had a phone system or something.

I could see it now. I closed my eyes and imagined calling him. Ring Ring. Hello Green Man, got a problem. The bees are dying, and we Keepers are trying to figure out why. Got any ideas? After all, you're supposed to be in charge of all that stuff, living creatures and all. I figure bees fall into that category. So what do you think?

I smiled as I settled into a more comfortable sleeping position. Brewford got more comfortable by readjusting himself to lie next to me. It felt safe to have his comforting lump of fur near me.

Then, I saw a bright light by the end of my bed. I blinked, but it didn't go away. It got brighter as it grew in size. It started to swirl and spin until it got as big as the bed, and still didn't stop growing. That's when I sat up. Something was happening and I didn't know what. I shook Brewford.

What, what is it? I am almost asleep. A groggy cat voice echoed in my mind.

"Brewford, something is happening at the foot of my bed."

Before I could thought-talk more, a golden spiraled horn appeared moving out through the opening of light. It was followed by a golden hoof, white shimmering fetlocks on a horse like creature so beautiful, it took my breath away. The mane was a sparkle of gold. Could it be?

The creature turned to face me, horn towards me. *Wanda, I am Chyra, your Unicorn Guide. The Green Man has heard your request for an audience, and I am to guide you to him.*

CHAPTER 6

The Fairy Paths

Okay, there was a unicorn standing in my bedroom. The unicorn's thoughts still twinkled in my mind. Its thoughts were like sparkles that left tingles along my temples. Its indigo eyes were lined with golden lashes, and its body looked equine. Yet, horse would be not a full description, since it's tail and mane were in a continuous flowing golden motion. Energy moved around it with a rainbow mist. It turned its head to the opening, with the light from the gateway glinting off its horn. Then it turned its head back, fixing one eye on me again.

Shall we? The unicorn thought spoke like Brewford directly into my mind.

"Ah, wait a sec. You're a unicorn, and the Green Man heard my call?"

Yes. It nodded. *You thought spoke your request, and the Green Man considers your situation urgent. He has given you an audience, and I am to guide you through the fairy paths to his fairy realm in Ireland.*

"You mean that thinking worked? He heard me? Wait a sec. He's in Ireland?"

It is the Green Man's home court and seat of power. Many Keepers throughout the Fairy World visit him there. Are you ready for your journey?

Now I took a moment. Blinking didn't make the unicorn go away. Is this still for real? Unicorns stepping into my room in a swirl of rainbow light had to be a dream, right? But since I had started helping the fairies, anything was becoming real, even unicorns. Vampires and werewolves could just be around the corner. I looked down at Brewford. He didn't have a look of sympathy, but more an 'I told you so" face.

He sat up a bit. *Did I forget to mention the Keeper Ability to mind speak great distances?*

I put my hands on my hips as he gave me a half-eyed stare. "Yes I think you did, Brew."

Thought it might not be necessary to let you know about that power. Never thought you'd finally ask for help again. But it's about time you did ask. The situation is getting crucial. Some Keepers think they can do it all themselves.

Well, at least he told me afterwards. So I could call the Green Man if needed. Who else could I call? I shook my head to look Brewford again.

I think I needed my sidekick again on this adventure. He didn't like that I called him that though. I put on my best pleading look, kind of like Puss'N'Boots in the movie "Shrek". "Can I ask for your help Brewford? I'd like to have your cat advice along for the ride. Could you come with me? I might need some helpful advice before I seem to need it."

He gave a quick cat upward stretch. *Granted. I will come.* He turned to the unicorn. *I beg your pardon Unicorn Chyra, may*

I ask for your assistance? It has been a while since I traveled the fairy paths. May I ride upon your back?

Yes, Friend Cat, in fact, you may both ride. It will be faster traveling the paths. Come, we must hurry. The Green Man cannot be kept waiting.

The unicorn went along the side of my bed, and I stepped over and onto its back. Brewford settled in front of me, sitting on his haunches. Unicorns were definitely wider than a horse. It was like floating on a pillow as the unicorn turned slowly and went through the opening.

We were on a path lined with crystals. It was similar to a tunnel, but lit by the unicorn's horn. Crystals embedded in the walls sparkled at me.

"Where are we?" I looked around and got more settled on the unicorn's back. It had been awhile since I'd ridden. Luckily, my Girl Scout troop had taken a field trip to a horse stable last summer. We had learned some of the basics of riding horses. But was riding a unicorn truly like riding a horse?

The unicorn's voice sounded more like bells than chimes as she continued. *The paths are tricky to leave and follow into other realms. The lines of energy follow the paths. I am an expert in following the magic that flows within the paths. It is why I am a guide.*

"Sounds like those ley lines I read about."

I do believe the human world has given the paths that name. The unicorn's voice sounded teacher like as she continued. *But in the World of Fairy, they are the paths of magic. They are much the same in the World of Humans. But once crossed into the World of Fairy, they are dangerous if one doesn't understand their flow.*

"I think I was learning about that before school started. Keepers can use energy from their fairy hill."

Yes, Fairy Hills are a power source. But the energy here is stronger. She dipped her head and I watched sparkles spill out of her horn and disappear into the distance. Rainbows dove past us and darted down different directions around us. *One must know how to direct the energy as you walk the paths.* The whole place felt alive with light and energy now.

We followed the yellow crystal path which now turned a corner. Ahead I could see a light. The hint of blue touched the corner of the openings.

The unicorn's voice in my head startled me. *We are approaching a crossing. You may have to hold on tight.*

"Crossing?"

Brewford chimed into our discussion with his smug cat tone. *A crossing is a place where energy meets and merges. It is similar to an ocean on Earth. Unicorns are experts at guiding through crossings. I don't think I could manage getting through that much energy on my own. After all, I am just a Cat Sorcerer. Unicorns are masters of navigating magic.*

"I thought you were a Master Sorcerer, Brewford?"

I felt his fur ruffle behind me. *I am. But unicorns are made of pure energy. They live on the fairy paths, and are creatures of Fairy. Very rarely do they enter into the World of Humans. It is an honor to ride upon one.*

"Brewford, I do think you sound humbled? Is it possible?"

It is an honor to be guided by a unicorn Wanda. Remember as much as you can about this experience.

I took a moment. I imagine riding on a unicorn's back can humble anyone. I felt relaxed and safe. I wasn't at all worried about the whooshing maelstrom of energy I heard ahead at the end of the tunnel. The crunching of gravel under Chyra's hooves matched the sway of her walk. I moved into balancing myself with her steady pace. The swish of her tail caught me once on my back. More crystals were loose upon the floor and a reflection sparkled as I looked down. Her hooves crunched along the path. Just ahead, the maelstrom of energy sounded like a river in a rage.

"How are we going to get through that?" I said out loud before thinking. It was that kind of outburst that used to get me in trouble in school.

Before I could say anything to cover myself, the unicorn answered. *Wishing to pass through the vortex of energy takes concentration on controlling the chaos within. Here, I will demonstrate.*

The unicorn closed its eyes. The maelstrom of energy seemed to slow. The rumbling of the unicorn's voice began to echo around us. *I command the chaos to find direction. Go to your direction of need. Follow your correct path. All chaos still.*

The swirls of light began to spin and flow off down different paths. Soon, the intersection was clear of most of the flows of energy. Wisps trickled around, circled my ankles and sped past the other side of the unicorn.

That is the correct way to find a way to end chaotic energy. You just need to give it some place to go. The unicorn nodded, her mane dancing about her face. She started to move forward through the intersection. As we past, I looked down some other tunnels and saw different lights winking in the distance. Different paths were lit with green, yellow, pink, purple, or blue. The intersection was a vertical cave with other higher openings above. More energy surged above us.

"What about up there?" I pointed to the upper levels of the intersection.

Those are the higher levels where other fairies and creatures of fairy travel. It would be more difficult for a human to travel the upper levels of the ley lines. The unicorn's voice sounded very stern, as if discouraging that line of questioning.

Human bodies are too dense in mass to travel. Brewford decided to add his two cents to the conversation. This was starting to sound like another lesson. *Your heavy body cannot travel that path while you are in the Human World.*

"Can I ever travel that path?" I was feeling disappointed. "I thought Keepers could do anything in the Fairy World."

There are limits, even for Keepers, Brewford continued. *Everyone must find his or her own limitations. But with much study, some humans have reached the higher levels. But it is very difficult.*

I nodded realizing I had a lot already to learn. "Maybe I should just stick to trying to save the fairies."

It is a wise decision. Many try to strive too high too soon. Waiting and facing what you need to learn right now is the first step to being a good Keeper. Brewford gave a slight snort to emphasize his point. *How much longer friend Unicorn?*

We must cross the Waters and then enter into the realm of the Green Man, answered the unicorn. *We are nearing the Waters now.*

I looked down and saw a creek bank with small, crystal points falling into a clear stream. The unicorn started across. Before long, the water seemed to stretch endlessly across, getting darker as we continued our pace.

The World of Fairy has no time. So as we progressed through the water, I had little thought except of what might be on the other side. What did the Green Man's realm look like? I didn't know much about Ireland. I knew it was near England and Scotland. It was full of history, castles, and I even had an ancestor who came from there during the Great Potato Famine in the 1840s.

But what if the Green Man didn't have the answer? What if I came all this way for nothing? I looked down at the water, and started to see swirling faces snarling back. They began to shape words. "Turn back Wanda. This is not your destiny." Another face continued the lament as I turned to see it. "Leave the path. Turn back. Turn back."

"Brewford, do you see that?" The faces started to blur.

Wanda, I'd appreciate it if you tried to think positive. Brewford seemed to be waking up from a dream swept sleep. He had curled into his sleeping ball position. *The Fairy World works on thoughts turning into reality. You're starting to turn your reality into being. Try to think positive.*

"You mean, all that in the water is my thoughts."

"Yes. Here, your thoughts become reality."

The unicorn's voice tinkled in my mind. *Wanda, were you perhaps looking at the water?*

"Yes, and then I started thinking about what might happen when I got to see the Green Man."

Then your thoughts turned the water into the reality you shaped it to, black and murky, with your worries swimming through out it. She swung around to turn an eye towards me. *I'd appreciate it if you turned the water back to a clear state again. It will be easier to navigate then.*

"But how do I do that?"

Brewford lifted his head. *Think positive Wanda. Then, the water will be filled with your positive thoughts.*

I looked down at the murky mess I had caused. Ok, concentrate, positive. Rainbows. Creeks with quartz and granite to climb on. Waterfalls. Springs.

The water started to change, as if all the dirt was settling to the bottom.

Think of the tadpoles I caught and put in my pond this summer. Getting an "A" on my quiz Friday, hopefully. The water seemed less murky now.

My favorite song by that band whose name I keep forgetting. Petting Brewford when I get home from school. The water was clear enough to see myself now.

Thank you Wanda. The unicorn gave a swish of her tail for emphasis. *Remember, thoughts have power, especially in the World of Fairy.*

We started to ascend up onto a bank of black sand. I could hear the crunch of the sand crystals against the hooves of the unicorn. A mist covered this side of the fairy path. We were no longer in a cave, but along a beach dotted with white stones and black sand.

The unicorn stopped. She tossed her head downward. *Here is where I must leave you. Unicorns cannot go much further into the World of Humans. The Green Man's court rests over that hill. Look for the entrance among the stone.*

I slid down from her back, crunching on the black sand. Brewford leaped down and started to lick his front paw.

The unicorn nodded and turned, walking slowly into the mist.

"But which way is the entrance?" I stammered as she turned.

There was no answer.

CHAPTER 7

An Uninvited Guest

So now what? I tried to shout at Chyra again, but she had disappeared into the haze. Mists swirled around my legs and arms. It was like early morning at the beach, when I had camped there a few times with Mom and Dad before the divorce. It was a low fog, and I couldn't see much except some cliffs around me. I must be on some lower beach below the cliffs. I wondered if there was a way up? I looked up to see that the rock faces were grey and sprinkled with green.

"So what now Brew? Shall we try to go up?" I looked up the craggy sides.

There might be a path near the cliffs. He started off towards the rocky edge. I tromped right behind him, not wanting to loose him in the murkiness.

"This isn't what I thought it was going to be like here?" I said to Brewford as he scampered along. It seemed a good idea to say it out loud. If thoughts were reality, maybe that's why it looked unexpected.

Ireland is a beautiful island, not only with hills of green, but with beaches, woods, and hills. Brewford's mind speech was strong, but it was so foggy I could barely see him.

I rushed to keep up with his tabby tail as a marker in the gloom. "You sound like you've been here before Brewford."

I did study here a while ago, under the instruction of Castrotomas. He is an elder Cat Sorcerer. The island is full of ancient power. It is wise to seek the Green Man here. All sources of power can be felt in Ireland. He stopped and started to swish his tail. *This is not the path I thought. Maybe we are on a beach that is further down than I've been before.*

A mysterious voice echoed from the cliff edge. "You may be right, or maybe things have been transformed since the last time you were here, friend cat."

Brewford looked up bristling his whiskers. There was a thump, as if something heavy landed behind me.

Turning about, I looked down to notice a small person, child-sized but with a grown-up face, a waistcoat and big floppy hat. His shoes had big silver buckles along with his hat, and he had a red beard. His green challenging eyes looked at me while his rose bud mouth turned into a smile. "At least, only a friend would be able to travel these paths. Especially with a cat sorcerer of such reputation."

Brewford's eyes grew wide. *Lubdan?* He gave the little man a sniff. *Is it you?* He moved forward and licked the small man on the hand. *It has been a long time.*

"About 100 years. But who is to say how long time is in the World of Fairy. It's been awhile since you've been in Ireland, Brewford."

The world is in troubled times. Brewford turned to me. *This is Lubdan, a Leprechaun Protector of the Emerald Isle. This is Wanda, a Crystal Keeper from the Western Realms.*

Lubdan gave me a tremendous bow, complete with hand sweep. "'Tis an honor my lady, to meet so worthy a friend. You are most welcome in the Fairy Realm of the Emerald Isle."

I bowed back. What else was I to do? I hadn't been given lessons on how to meet a leprechaun yet. But I stuck to normal social niceties. "Nice to meet you." I extended my hand in a handshake.

"I've heard of this custom. You grab it like so." He looked to Brewford who nodded. He gave it a good shake, pumping my hand each word. "I-am-glad-to-meet-you!"

"No problem Lubdan, but once is enough." Then it hit me. "Wait, Brewford, the last time you were here was 100 years ago? How old are you?"

He gave a shake of his tail. *863 years I believe, give or take a year. After 500, it's harder to keep track.* My look must have driven him to continue. *Don't look so startled Wanda. Cat Sorcerers are immortal until their mission on Earth is done. I've only maybe gotten through half my mission. Still many more Crystal Keepers to train, including you.* He winked at me and turned to Lubdan. *We are in need of the Green Man's wisdom in a Keeper situation. May we ask you to lead us to the entrance to his realm?"*

"But of course friend cat, I will be honored. For a friend is most welcomed, and an enemy welcomed, but watched." He gave me a big wink, and walked up a trail that had not been there before. We followed after, trying to do double steps to keep up with the leprechaun's quick pace.

He headed up the narrow path covered in a green blanket of clovers. I had a chance to spot the number of leaves. I glanced down and noticed a four-leaf clover among the others. An impulse over took me to pluck it. I remembered what Broc has said that sometimes the Fairy World made you feel compelled towards things you would need. So, I put it in my jacket pocket. Never could hurt to have a little portable luck.

When I was done, I looked up to see both of them gone. "Brewford? Brewford?" What was the leprechaun's name again? I'm so bad with names. "Leprechaun…friend? Where did you disappear to?"

The mists swirled around me. I couldn't see down or up. The swirling turned green and black. A voice started to speak within the mist in front of me.

"Turn back Wanda. You will never find what you seek. Travel the Fairy Path no longer." The voice echoed backwards into the fog and formed a shadow in front of me. The shadow figure formed into a man shape with red eyes. Glistening spaces in the maw of its mouth seemed pointed into a smile. Then he formed into a pale, thin man. He had on a grey and dark purple robe that swirled about him. He held a large walking stick, which could have passed for any wizard's staff. His pale complexion made him look sick and ill humored. He started to twirl his thin, black mustache. " So we meet at last." His nasal voice echoed in my mind after he spoke.

I tried not to smile as the thought came to me and answered, "No, at first." If this was the Green Man, maybe he had a sense of humor. "And you are the Green Man I presume?" There, that sounded straight from a movie. I might be getting this hero thing right after all.

He only gave me a smile and said, "No, I wouldn't presume to be him. I'm someone much more important to you."

He didn't seem overly friendly, and there was something not right about him. This guy just seemed down right creepy. Maybe he was another kind of trap. He made my skin feel prickly as he looked at me.

Then, I remembered the clover. I held it in my pocket and it tingled. Maybe there was something to the luck being in a four-leaf clover.

"You will let me pass." I felt bolder. "For it is my choice." I reached in my pocket and rubbed the clover in my coat pocket. "I don't have time to deal with super, spooky wannabe shadows." I started to walk past him.

"Wanda, surely you know not what faces you." He blocked my path. "I am who you seek."

"Oh come on! I've heard better lines in most horror films. You've got to do better than that." I went to walk past and he blocked the way in front of me. "I've faced shadows before. You were never real." I tried again, and he took two steps back with me.

He seemed to rise up a bit in front of me and said, "I do remember how you faced my allies in the real world. But now, you are in the World of Fairy. And here, fear can become reality in the speck of an instant." His red eyes gleamed down. "We will meet again. Luck is with you today, for I cannot touch you with a charm of the Fairy Realm held within your hand. But..."

He leaned forward. I could smell his stink like a strong whiff of a cat box right after usage. "We will meet again; sooner than you think."

A whoosh of black mist ended his words stronger than a period. I was waiting for the whoosh of fire to come up like in the Wizard of Oz. But there was only a strong wind with the scent of rotten leftovers.

Wanda? Wanda? Brewford swept through the murkiness to me. *Where have you been?* His whiskers were smoothed back against his face. They started to lower some when he continued, along with the fur on his back. He even looked concerned. *We lost you in the fog. And then Balkazaar appeared.*

"We thought for the worst, friend Keeper." Lubdan rushed up next to him. His hat was gripped in his hand as if he had been running with it. "Were you frightened with the Master of Shadow Sorcerers blocking the path? We thought surely he would do away with you."

I noticed a shiver escape my shoulders as I pulled out the four-leaf clover. It was a bit crumpled now, but still whole. "I don't know what really happened back there, but I know one thing, I definitely had a bit of luck."

Chapter 8

The Hidden Cave

*W*e shall not dally, I think. Whenever the Shadow Sorcerer *appears, it is best to leave the area as soon as possible. Negative energy always remains behind.* Brewford swished his tail as if to emphasis his point.

I started to feel this overwhelming sense of depression. Like from all sides, there was no hope to go forward or back. It all just seemed pointless.

"Brewford, I think you're right."

As usual. He sounded smug as he slinked off through the disappearing mists.

"After you my lady." Lubdan pointed in the direction in which I could see a tabby tail held high. I nodded and went after the cat. Flanked by leprechaun and cat, we followed a narrow trail through the forest. It was so green, I wondered if it was an illusion. Leaves drifted slowly down upon a slight breeze. Flowers nestled among different variations of bushes and twigs. Blackberries intertwined with ripe fruit. It was a bounty of vegetation flung among boulders of granite and a greenish marble.

"You seem to be admiring our forest Keeper." Lubdan piped up. He followed my eyes to the stone.

"I haven't seen rocks like that before." I pointed to a large section of rock on the side of the path.

"It is very special to the land of Eire. It is called Connemara Marble. It is a greenish marble found only in this area of the Fairy World and the Real World. It marks the region for our Fairy Realm. It is special to the Green Man since it is partly the power storage of his region."

"Like quartz?" I remembered reading about how quartz crystal could conduct electrical energy.

"The same. It is very similar and is found throughout the Green Man's Realm. The land of Eire, or Ireland is what I think you humans call it, is the only place that it can be found."

I picked up a small piece to look at it closer. The piece was half green and half tan. It had veins of dark stone running through it like moss agate. Here and there was a chunk of quartz. It was smoothed around the edges. A tingle went through my fingers.

"The stone is calling you. There must be a need for you to take it with you." Lubdan touched it lightly. "You should take it with you. Sometimes stones can be your guide with the Earth. It might be able to tell you something if you concentrate."

"Maybe later. We've got to catch up or we'll loose Brewford." I tucked it in my pocket and started to give a little run to catch up with my cat. I heard the patter of boots on the path behind me. Looking behind, I saw Lubdan hopping along to keep up as well. "You're not what I thought a leprechaun would be like Lubdan," I said when he reached me. "Like, where is your pot of gold?"

Lubdan made a face. "Tis' a wise tale. I have not one place for any gold I acquire through my cobbling. I have many stashes of my gold and wares."

"Cobbling?"

"Shoe making, my dear Keeper. Most leprechauns are master shoe makers." He pointed to his shoes. "These I made for myself. Nice fit and fine fairy silver. We deplore most metals but gold and silver. I need to keep a stash of gold and silver around the world to make most of my shoe wares. Fairies are sensitive to all metals but those two. Plus, I get paid with gold for my wares. Next time you need a pair of shoes Wanda, let me know. I've not had a Keeper to make shoes for in at least 100 years." He winked at me and I winked back.

Not far now. Brewford sent a quick shout to my mind. *Just a bit further and the opening should be around the next bend.*

The path led downward and was strewn with more green marble. The quartz veins sparkled when we reached a clearing. Here I could see vast coverings of shamrocks all around the ground and going up the cliff side. Butterflies landed on the pink flowers among the clovers.

I think this is it, said Brewford as he came to a stop just as the cliff side went upward. I looked around for some kind of door. All I could see was a narrow opening in the rock, barely enough for me to get through. The marble rock came close together to form a slit only about two feet wide.

"After you Brew. You seem to know the way." I felt uneasy as I looked at the opening. "It doesn't look like I'll fit."

"You'll have to trust that you will. I don't think the Green Man gets many human visitors. So you may have to duck most of the way." Lubdan took off his hat. "Sometimes even leprechauns do too. Are you afraid of being in narrow places?"

I shook my head. "I don't think so, why?" Then again? Maybe I was a little nervous. I didn't like being that closed in.

I must have had a scared look because Lubdan answered, "It gets really narrow in some places. You might have to walk sideways. Thought I could warn you as we go ahead." He ducked past me and went through the opening.

Brewford blinked at me while he stood at attention. *I'll come behind. It's best Lubdan leads to announce that you've arrived. Different realms have more pomp and circumstance. The old kingdoms tend to be more oriented that way.*

I bit my lip a bit to take a moment. It didn't look too bad. I started forward after Lubdan holding onto the edge of the rock. That made me feel more steady. Once through the front of the opening, it turned into a narrow downward passage complete with wooden staircase.

My feet scuffed the wood as I went downward. The edges of rock came right to the sides of my face. The stairway was steep and I held onto the walls to keep steady. It started to feel stuffy. Sunlight lit the passage until we started going down. Then, the walls started to glow slightly. The veins of quartz within the marble started to glow. After several flights and two turns, we came to a level passage.

Ahead was a spiral staircase of silver. It had a cage-like outer structure for a railing as it spiraled downward into a vertical cave chamber. "No one mentioned anything about this." I peered down the staircase that was only surrounded by darkness as it continued onward. "NO WAY!" I clung to the edge of the brim. I started to feel dizzy. "Brewford, it's not going to be possible for me to even do this."

Lubdan looked back. "Trouble my lady?"

"You didn't mention anything about cliffs and edges."

"I didn't think there was a need, friend Keeper. Is this a fear you harbor?"

I looked down the staircase. The silver steps twisted in a perfect circle around a central pillar. The railing was encased by an ingenious cage-like structure. It kind of looked safe. But I still didn't think I could do it. My legs were shaking as I neared the edge. I backed up and held the wall again. This was a challenge I didn't know if I could do it. I was thinking of going back up. Really. It was that much of a drop.

Wanda... Brewford's voice was soothing. *You've got to try. This is the only way into the Green Man's Chamber. Try to think of a way to face your fear.*

I closed my eyes and could imagine myself plummeting down the sides. I wasn't scared when I did trampoline or walked the beam. So how come I felt this way when I was near an edge? I could feel my fingers digging at the grit on the wall. I started thinking about Eddie. What would she do if she were here? She always seems to be more confident than me.

I had to do this. I had to be as good a Keeper as Eddie. But do what? How could I get down safely? Then, I looked at the railing. "Maybe I can go slow and hold the railing."

I took the first step onto the staircase. The polished surface of the railing was smooth and cool. One step at a time, I went down the stairs. There, one step. Then another step.

"Hey, once I've started, it's not so difficult," I shouted back to Brewford following behind me.

Most challenges are often hardest to start Wanda. Brewford was using his teaching voice again. *One step at a time is the best way to face any challenge.*

I looked down at the steps. "Yeah, literally one step at a time Brew." I laughed.

One slow breath, one step. One slow breath, one step. As I kept going, I tried not to look out into the chamber. One step, one breath. One step, one breath.

Then, after a while, I looked outward. I was careful to look only outward, because looking down would have been too much. I saw the faint outlines of stalactites and large stone formations. The one directly across was all white where water had dripped downward for eons. It looked like a mushroom with its white plume melting downward. Another looked like a giant pillar going downward into the chamber. Another on the far side was mostly all brown, like a chocolate waterfall.

I kept going down. The light was even throughout, with the silver reflecting the glow from the nearby walls. Finally, I reached the opening at the bottom of the staircase. I went through the cage doorway and entered the bottom of the cave chamber. I could look up at the formations and felt like I'd accomplished something. I did it. I'd made it safely to the bottom.

A voice echoed from somewhere in front of me. "Very good Wanda. Sometimes the first step is the hardest. But in the end, you will find that you can do anything if you don't give up."

CHAPTER 9

The Green Man

The voice came from an alcove at the base of the stairs. I couldn't see who had spoken, but I heard the rustling of leaves as steps came forward. He came into the glow of the rocks, The Green Man, or least it had to be. I'd not seen anyone completely made of leaves, flowing towards me on a breeze. His steps were like a ballet. Each one carefully placed with purpose. His eyes were an emerald green, with his face hidden behind a beard of leaves. His hair of twigs and leaves seemed untamed.

His arms had branches of ivy coming out of the sleeves of a green tunic. The sleeves were long and wide like pictures of a Celtic tunic in the Ireland book back in the crystal shop. A belt of silver glinted through the foliage at his waist with a silver band around his neck. The necklace looked like a torque necklace in the Ireland book. Torques were round, thick bands that were like necklaces. The Irish Chieftains wore them to show status. It definitely fit him.

He had a warm smile with green lips, but his teeth were a gleaming gold. He looked as steady as an oak tree, as he looked right at me.

The Green Man motioned me forward. "Come. We have much to talk about." I followed him as we made our way across the chamber. He directed me to sit on a large stone chair next to him. He sat upon a throne-like chair of green marble.

"Here is my audience chamber." The Green Man gestured about. "You are most welcome in these grievous times. Crystal Keepers are losing their ground against the darkness. We need so much help from all of you."

I looked around at the chamber. The smell of damp assaulted my nostrils. As I looked around, water dripped down the light and dark marbled walls. The drip, drip rhythm seemed to calm me. I started to feel more comfortable, even though I was sitting on a stone chair. Luckily, there were notches to rest my arms. I started to ease back and feel less nervous.

The Green Man leaned a little towards me. "Now, what is it that you need? I could hear your call strongly across the waters that divide us. It must be quite troublesome."

I nodded again. He had a very imposing way of looking and speaking. His voice would boom outward making it hard to concentrate. But I gathered up my speaking courage and remembered again; I was a Keeper. "The bees are dying where I live Green Man. I can call you that, right?"

He gave me a gentle smile. "It is my most common name."

I swallowed. "So, I was looking up stuff in this crystal store back home. And found some things written about you." I looked again to make sure he was following along. He nodded to continue. "So, then I saw things that mentioned that you were in charge of nature and maybe you might know what was happening with the bees."

"They are the most helpful creatures, one of the only insects that heeded my call to aid the Fairy Kingdoms." He looked down deep in thought. "I have felt their energy waning, and not known why."

"Really? You were noticing something was wrong too?"

"Yes, your call only confirmed my suspicions. For I have known the energies of my bee friends to be in trouble. I have been trying to trace the source myself, but have found none. I am afraid I can give you no answer, friend Keeper." He put his hand under his beard looking deep in thought.

I waited for an answer. He just sat there thinking. "But you are suppose to know all the answers with nature?" Ok, so I blurted it out. I couldn't help it.

He began to laugh, a big bellow that echoed through the cavern. "What myth is this? No creature on Earth has all of the answers. If we did, we would not be in search of constant knowledge."

"But the books said..."

"Do not worry about written facts and information. They are only a guide to the knowledge you may seek. That can be limiting at times. Often, you must search for an understanding of what you are seeking."

I sighed. It seemed to help, to steady me. I took a deep breath to help me focus. It's something the elves had taught me during the summer. "I thought you'd definitely know what to do. You seemed to be the smartest. "

He paused looking like a statue. "Do not limit yourself to just one person for help. Wisdom lies in seeking out the knowledge to solve your problem. I will try to do what I can to help you. Maybe if we work it out together, something may become apparent."

"Okay." I smiled and added, "But where do we start?"

"That is always the hardest part of any problem." He turned to me with a growing grin. "But sometimes the best way to get started is to start moving." He grabbed my hand. "I think there is someone we can consult in this matter. That will give us a beginning."

I felt the whoosh of being raised forward, like flying on a roller coaster with no bottom. We were sailing through the air, going by corridors and long tunnels with howling winds. Leaves blew behind us as we traveled. Dust flew about my face, and I tried to block it with my arm to keep my eyes open.

I wondered what had happened to Lubdan and Brewford. The Green Man was really daunting, but I didn't think Brew was scared of anything. Or maybe he'd done what cats mostly do, disappeared when you wanted to know where he was. But I doubted the leprechaun was scared. He had led me to the Green Man after all.

My thoughts stopped when I saw the opening ahead. I still felt like I was in the middle of a storm. Suddenly, there was a light ahead. The corridor started to glow from its crystal quartz sides. Gold veins etched through the corridor as if pointing ahead. I heard another maelstrom of energy. But I didn't have time to think or even be scared as the Green Man whisked me through it. His arm was the only stable element keeping me in place through the whirlwind of energy. Then we turned right.

We whooshed out of the cave and into the forest. High above the treetops, we flew as if on a breeze. The sun was setting in the distance, and I could see for miles around. In the distance, I saw hills of emerald green.

"Your Fairy World is so beautiful Green Man."

"Aye, it is. But we have entered the Real World now of Eire. We are in Ireland now."

I looked down at the green hillsides. The book had mentioned Ireland was the Emerald Isle. I could see why. Waves of jade swept below me. Mists trailed in the spaces between, and small creeks danced below. It was like a fairy tale land. But then, didn't some fairy tales come from Ireland? That could mean fairies were in other places that had fairy tales like Germany and France? And were they all over the World?

I didn't have long to wonder since the whooshing and scenery kept distracting me from my thoughts. I kept looking down at the small houses and roadways. I could see some woods surrounding some of the towns, and in some cases, fields with sheep, cows, and haystacks.

It was like in that cartoon movie I remember seeing in preschool. This little boy is taken on an adventure with a snowman, and he flies over the world by night. It felt like that kind of an adventure. Which also brought up another point? If I could be flying with the Green Man over Ireland, would it be possible someday to hang out with Santa Claus?

I didn't have time to rework my vision of the world quite yet, for the Green Man had started a descent into a grove of oak trees. Haze was blocking a view of the area below us. We swept down, our bodies lowering feet first, until I could run along the ground with the Green Man.

"There we go. We can run to a stop now," he boomed with enthusiasm. "Careful when you stop. You might feel somewhat light-headed."

I followed the Green Man's pace until we were safely "landed". Then I felt a sudden lethargic feeling come over me. Wow. I had to hold onto my sides. I felt suddenly like I'd run a race.

Levitation is related to running. Takes about the same amount of energy.

I heard the thought talk plainly as a bell in my head, but didn't recognize who it was. I turned to see a strange cat sitting under one of the trees. He was a grey and white tabby with golden eyes. Standing next to him was Brewford. The Green Man came up from behind me and placed a hand on my shoulder.

The Green Man's voice boomed with humor as he said, "May I introduce some friends of mine Wanda."

Brewford's familiar mind speech continued the conversation in my mind. *It's about time you showed up Wanda. Sometimes meetings can take awhile, but Castrotomas and I have been waiting a goodly time. The situation is worse than we thought.*

And it may affect all of the Fairy Kingdoms, continued the strange cat. *Unless it's already too late.*

CHAPTER 10

Secrets Revealed

I followed them through the grove into a large oak tree. Really, that was no surprise. I was even getting used to the hollow feeling as you stepped through tree doorways. We came into what looked like a cross between a workroom and a booth at a Renaissance Faire. Old looking parchments and books were lying around on large carved tables. Small stools were set by most of them. Shelves lined the walls with corked bottles, wooden boxes, and more books. One window let in masked sunlight. It reminded me of the cookie elves commercial on TV. Of course, everything looked antique and not like a cartoon.

The strange cat led the way to one corner of the room in which he jumped up onto a stool. His tail drooped off the edge. Brewford popped up on the other end of the table, looking towards the strange cat.

Now, if we could try to get started. The strange cat's head voice began. *I'll start dictating what I see in the seeing crystal. Brewford my boy, you can take notes.* His thought talk had a slight English lilt or accent.

"I'm sorry, I don't want to be rude. But what are we doing? And who are you?" I looked at the cat with hands on my hips. Ok, maybe not so polite, but I tried. I also hate being bossed around. If anything, I'd learned you can't let your cat do that for too long. They'll walk all over you later.

Oh, I beg your pardon. The strange cat looked back at me. He now had a pair of round wire-rimmed glasses perched on his nose. *I am Castrotomas. I usually don't waste time with introductions. But I forgot how fond you humans are of them.*

"Okay, well, it's a start," I said as I looked at the Green Man and he grinned back. "I'm guessing that the crystal thing can help with the bee problem."

Bee problem and the greater problem at large, yes. He turned back to his crystal sphere on the table. It was a large crystal ball, with blue and purple swirls. It was the same color as some fluorite crystals in the Crystal Shop back home. The strange cat, the one who called himself Castrotomas, looked at the crystal. Well, ok, he began to gaze, intently. We waited. And waited. And waited. Nothing. He didn't move.

Okay, a case of the fidgets started to hit me then. It seemed like an hour had gone by and all I'd been doing was sitting on a stool like forever. Well, maybe it was only about 10 minutes. But I'm used to moving from time to time. So, I got up and started looking at books on the shelves around me.

As the others watched Castrotomas stare at the crystal, I picked one shelf to look over. It was near the window so I could read them clearly. Strange titles scripted in gold or silver writing ran along the edges of the bindings. "Binding the Shadows". "Spells to Save the World". "Wrinkles in the

Universe: A Full Map" "Time as our Travel Friend", and the last strange title, "The Cat Sorcerer's Guide to the Universe".

I looked back to see if my friends had moved. Brewford gave a twitch with his ear, and the Green Man had settled into a chair. Adults can find the most boring things to keep themselves occupied.

"Anything yet," I shouted back placing "The Wrinkles of the Universe" back on the shelf.

Shhhh! Brewford's mind voice was harsh. *Castrotomas needs to concentrate while he gazes.*

"But why are we waiting?" I gave a little huff. I was feeling a bit trapped, like in study hall 10 minutes before the bell rings. It's like forever.

"Sometimes I think we forget she is still a child." The Green Man's voice boomed with sympathy. "Is there something you can have her help with while you look for breaks in the Energy Paths, Castrotomas?"

Castrotomas looked up from the table. *Actually, no. I need her to gaze into the ball now. The situation needs a Crystal Keeper's touch.*

"Huh?" was my only reply.

You are the Keeper we've been waiting for to handle the situation. You are the one with the ability to see the energies. You just don't know it yet. Castrotomas paused for a moment. *Come here. I will show you.*

What else could I do? I was definitely getting the Yoda feeling from this strange cat, but with an even stranger accent. "Ok, what do I do?" There, that sounded ready. But I felt my stomach do a somersault. I knew this was going to come down to me doing something that was going to make me earn the title of heroine, whether I liked it or not. My stomach still flipped as I walked over to stand by the crystal sphere. "Sometimes it's better to just get it over with."

"Acceptance is always the first sign of strength." Castrotomas sat up straighter on his stool and leaned towards me. *"First, clear your mind of all thoughts."*

I gave a deep breath like what I'd been practicing with the elves.

"Now center your thoughts on the calm place within you. Follow what the elves taught you."

I closed my eyes and imagined the beach. That was always my calm place. White sand. Palm trees. Clear light blue water lapping on the shore. The waves falling over and over until the rhyme calmed me. There was nothing else but the beach. Beach…ah.

"Now open your eyes slowly and gaze into the crystal."

His voice was an upset to the rhythm for a moment, only a moment. For when I stared into the crystal, I felt like I was falling down another hole. My mind sped with the fall, tickling parts of my temples. I could feel a rush of air, and suddenly there was a picture in my mind.

"Bees. Dead bees everywhere." I said what I was seeing out loud for everyone. "I see a patch of them near the edge of a cave."

The picture continued as I walked along the path following the dead bees. Then I heard a hum within the cave. The smell of a full garbage can wafted to my nose. Greenish sparks emitted through the opening as I turned the corner to enter. Darkness engulfed me. But the picture was still there, with green sparks drawing me forward.

I shook my head and the picture was still there. It was the man I'd met on the trail to the Green Man's cave. "That's it Wanda. Come to me." The voice was too spooky to be anyone else's. The voice belonged to Balkazaar.

I closed my eyes. I couldn't keep looking into the crystal sphere.

What is it Wanda? What did you see? Brewford's thought voice held waves of concern.

It's important to remember every detail, Castrotomas added.

"Well, it was so fast. But there were a lot of bees. Dead bees." I closed my eyes to remember. "And there was a cave with green sparks. Then a voice said 'Come to me.' I saw the man that stopped me on the path before!"

Brewford and Castrotomas gave each other a look.

The Green Man's voice echoed as he spoke, "I do propose this has the pattern of someone we've known for quite awhile Castrotomas."

Castro answered, *It must be Balkazaar. This is most disconcerting. Yet not surprising. We had suspected Balkazaar was behind everything to begin with.* Castrotomas turned towards me. *You have to gaze again and see if you can tell us what else you see. We need more clues.* He nodded downward, looking at me directly over his glasses.

"But it's hard concentrating with the smell and noise." I didn't want to go back into that cave. It was worst than having to get my homework done.

We need to know how he is killing the bees Wanda. We can't take the chance to NOT stop him, interrupted Brewford. His ears were lowered and he looked on the alert for trouble. *He is about mischief, utterly. And must be stopped at all cost. It was a dark day when he escaped the prison the Great Oak Council set for him.*

"What's the Great Oak Council?" I asked curious. "That's what Queen Alira mentioned she was a part of?" I was getting tired of asking questions with few answers.

"Yes Wanda, but all answers in good time." The Green Man answered me. His echoing voice turned gentle. "Now, we must find out if we can locate him. That means it's up to you Wanda. To find him."

I couldn't help it. I shook my head. "Oh no, not again. Why does this always happen to me?"

Because you're a Keeper. Brewford thought-talked back. *That comes with a certain amount of responsibility.*

I was thinking it would be easier to finish a book report. "But I'm not a grown-up. This just seems so much bigger than me. I mean, what did I ever do to this guy, Balkazaar? You said this council imprisoned him for some reason. Maybe he's a little mad about that." I put my hands on my hips. "Why don't they do something about it?"

The Green Man looked sad as he began to speak. "Because there are too few of us left. Some of the Fairy Queens and leaders of the other Fairy Kingdoms survived, but many did not."

Most of them were destroyed imprisoning Balkazaar in the first place, interrupted Castrotomas. *It took a lot of life energy to pull enough power to create the trap that kept him between worlds. Now that he is free, there aren't enough of us to put him back.* Castrotomas got down off of his stool. *Maybe it is time to tell you some answers Wanda. Rupert, where is the 'History of Human and Cat Sorcery'?*

A strange tabby came through a small opening between the bookcases. He looked over the bookshelves in a corner and then turned back. *It's not here Master. I thought you lent it to one of the Hawaiian Cat Masters last month.* His thought speech had an Irish lilt.

Fine, remarked Castro. *Stay Rupert. I may need you for assistance in finding more volumes.*

The strange assistant cat bowed and moved to sit near Brewford on a neighboring stool.

Castro's whiskers bristled and lowered. He took a deep breath. *I'll tell you some of it myself.* Castrotomas sat up a little straighter and took a deep breath. *It began long ago when humans were part of the Fairy World. The worlds were joined back then. The creatures of Fairy and the Real World crossed freely back and forth. There were very little boundaries between the worlds.*

Then, as the humans grew stronger, so did their weaknesses. They started to create war amongst themselves, starved for the greed that consumed them. They started to not look at the Earth as their friend, but as something to use and consume. This distanced their fairy allies. The Fairy World started to retreat from the Real World. To save itself, The World of Fairy hid to keep a connection to guard the Earth.

I added quickly, "That's why no one remembers anyone like the Green Man, except as a Legend, right?" I was starting to catch on to this hidden knowledge stuff. Maybe there was more to history and legends than just the stories.

The Green Man nodded. "The Fey, or fairy beings, created mists between the worlds that became a boundary to protect them from the World of Man. It can now only be crossed by the Fairy Ley Lines or paths, but only special creatures such as the unicorns are able to handle the energies necessary to cross over."

Or very powerful fairies or sorcerers. This is our concern, Castrotomas added. *But let's continue. Next, the dark sorcerers appeared; humans that transformed themselves from captured fairy magic. They were challenged by the Elves, and their allies, the Cat Sorcerers. A war ensued, and was won by the Warriors of Light lead by the Elves and Cat Sorcerers.*

The dark sorcerer leader, Balkazaar, was imprisoned between the worlds to keep him from returning to start another war. But his bonds are growing weak as the Real World destroys the energies of the Earth. Pollution is robbing the Fairy World of power, and the bonds are slipping. His evil is emerging slowly to influence the world. I tried to warn the remaining council members that the bonds were weakening. But it didn't help.

"There was nothing to be done", insisted the Green Man. "They are all too set in their old ways. If he breaks free, we all could be undone."

Castrotomas took another deep breath ending with a long sigh. *Yes, I agree. The discussion has frustrated me for some time. But to continue.*

We found that some humans had the ability to manipulate fairy magic. The ability seemed to be the most potent during the years they were children. So we enlisted these children sorcerers to become our Keepers, to guard the entrances between the World of Fairy and the Real World. But since the Dark Sorcerer was trapped there, he could sense these young Keepers. He found a way to harness their power to help him escape. We believe that he needs a lot of power to continue.

"That's what must have happened to Jordan when he got trapped in the shadow maze. Balkazaar could sense his power", I added.

Castrotomas nodded. *That is why it is so dangerous for you. He can sense your power. All sorcerers can sense each other. But then, that means you could sense him. He is getting stronger. I can feel it. If we do not find how he is gaining power, he will burst free into the Real World. And then there will be no stopping the Shadows from freely roaming our Earth again.*

"Again? What happened the first time?" I felt the surprise come out undisguised.

"Orcs and trolls roamed the Earth," answered the Green Man. "Along with other dark fairies, but many have now disappeared, or gone into hiding. If Balkazaar emerged again, they would come to aid him as minions."

I laughed. "Sounds almost too much like Middle Earth was real or something?"

They all looked at me. The Green Man answered. "How do you know it wasn't? Many truths are hidden within the fiction you read."

I took a moment. Real trolls and orcs? I know the special effects in movies were good these days. But from what I'd seen of real fairy creatures, the movies were not even close to the real fairies I'd met. Real trolls and orcs would be bad, very bad.

I squeezed my eyelids to release the tears that had started. I felt so immature. Here I was doing an adult thing because adults didn't have the power to do it. Kids did. Kids had the ability to draw the power the fairies needed, and I was one of them. How could I not help? And if we didn't do it soon, Balkazaar would enter the Real World.

I took a deep breath and asked, "So if he's building power somehow, we just have to find it, right?"

Yes, before he builds up enough energy to enter the Real World. Castro sounded hopeful. *Most Fairies have to change form. He would have enough power to remain a Sorcerer. And then he could use his magic to create the creatures of Shadow he had before the war. Trolls, Orcs, and Goblins.*

Goblins, I've read are especially vile, piped in Rupert, the apprentice cat.

Yes, and cats tend to be their favorite food, Castrotomas added.

I saw both Brewford and the apprentice cat bristle.

Brewford turned to me. *So Wanda, it comes down to you to help us find Balkazaar. I don't really want to be on the menu for goblins and trolls.*

Yes, friend Keeper. Castrotomas continued in a serious tone. *He is somewhere between the Real World and Fairy World, and he must be found. Somehow he is using the Ley Lines to draw power, and I'm guessing the bees are the key. Find the bees, and we will find him.*

I clenched my hands. There was only one simple solution. "It comes down to me."

"Yes Wanda," stressed Castrotomas, "unless it's already too late."

CHAPTER 11

Priorities

"So, how come it always comes to me? Aren't there other Keepers?" I mean, how come it's my turn to save the Fairy World again. I didn't ask for this. I never did. If I could take myself back to the day in the orchard when I first followed the crow out of curiosity, maybe I wouldn't have followed him through the opening in the trunk of the Oak Tree. I'd be safe, at home, not having to worry about stupid scary ole' dark sorcerers that will just as soon drain me of energy and steal my powers.

I looked for support first to Brewford, the Green Man, and Castrotomas. The Green Man was quiet in the back of the study-like room, sitting in an overly stuffed easy chair in the corner. Its burgundy leather had bits of stuffing coming out the sides. But he at least looked comfortable. I wished I felt that way.

Wait. Maybe that was it. If I was worried about him stealing my powers, maybe that is what he was doing. Either from other Keepers like Jordan before in the shadow maze, or maybe other keepers.

"Maybe he's stealing the powers from others still?" My outburst ended the silence.

Or other fairies. He could use their powers while holding them captive. It's so simple why didn't I think of it? stammered Castrotomas.

I put my hands on my hips. I was thinking it wasn't a simple idea, but brilliant. But I held my tongue. After all, we still had to figure out how.

I pushed the glasses back on my nose. "I think I might know a clue. The dead bees have got to link us to how he's stealing the energy. I think he's stealing power, I don't know how, but I think the green sparks might be another clue too. It's just too weird not to be."

Castrotomas blinked once. *Then there is only one thing to do. We must gaze again for the dark sorcerer. But we may have to shield our searching so he doesn't know we are looking. That calls for a different type of crystal all together.* He hopped down and went over to another shelf and hopped onto the stool in front of it. He peered intently at a shelf and slowly a box began to levitate off of it. It lowered down and he looked within. He snorted a bit smugly, and hopped down. The box levitated behind him.

I tried not to act surprised. I mean, he was a sorcerer. But it was still odd seeing the box follow him and onto the table as he sat back on the stool. *Wanda, if you reach within, you will find a new seeing crystal. This one is specially protected for this kind of far seeing.*

I followed his directions and leaned forward reaching within the box. I felt about over a couple of objects. Most were different like shells or long sticks, and then I felt the crystal. It was bigger than the other sphere. I pulled it out and looked at it. It was all yellow quartz with rainbows inside. I always like those the best. It had a little frost making it have different planes within that caused rainbows to show when turning it.

"Is this the right one?" I said showing Castrotomas the sphere.

"Yes, shall we begin again?"

I nodded and began my slow progression back to my calming place. The beach began to appear in my mind, sitting by the waves and the sun shining on my face. The heat and warmth relaxed me as I curled my toes in the sand. I looked into the crystal.

In an instant, everything else was gone and all I could see in my mind was the cave again. This time it was stronger in detail. The dead bees were still everywhere. Then I saw a live bee approach and saw it get whooshed into the cave by the wind. I heard a scream as I followed the bee through the mouth of the cave.

I focused on the bee as it glided through. I could see riding upon it a very small fairy. She looked terrified, pulling on reins that were attached to the bee's head. She was pulling frantically as the bee kept moving forward. I saw her continue forward despite her attempts to pull the bee to another direction. Then, she screamed. I focused to turn on what she saw.

Ahead of her loomed a large box glowing with streams of green sparks flowing outward. One of the green sparks grabbed her and pulled her forward. I watched her get pulled into the box and the bee slammed against the outside. It slid down lifeless.

I figured it was hitting with a force like that. Other bees were being pulled after another all hitting the box with no fairy riders. Then, a bit later, another bee with a fairy appeared. She was screaming louder than the other as she was pulled into the box. The bee died with a crunch as it hit the side. I heard the sound of a sizzle. It was like when flies hit those insect lights and get zapped. I tried not to cry. It was horrible to watch the scene of one bee after another getting zapped. Then, a wind came up blowing the bee bodies out of the cave.

I drew myself out of the vision and blinked. "Horrible. Absolutely horrible."

"What is it?" The Green Man was standing near me looking concerned.

"It was a giant green box trapping fairies and killing their bees that they rode. It was horrible. They would scream before entering and the bees would die when they hit the outside. We've got to stop it."

"It is as we feared," boomed the Green Man. "It appears the Dark Sorcerer is capturing Pillywiggin fairies to gather enough energy to escape."

"Pillywiggin fairies?" I asked surprised.

"Yes, they are the fairies that ride bees and are the guardians of wildflowers," answered The Green Man.

The type of flower fairy I told you earlier of, Wanda. Brewford looked smug. *I had suspected something might be connected with them.*

"How can he use the fairies?" I asked. I mean, were they just captured. "He can't make them, can he?"

Brewford started with his lecture voice. *He can keep them in prison and siphon their powers storing the power in different ways. Stones, rocks and even crystals can store fairy energy very nicely. With enough stolen fairy energy, it could shatter his prison once and forever.*

"What if he had a Keeper?" I didn't want to think of myself in the place of the fairies. "It doesn't hurt them, does it?" Or for that matter, would it hurt a Keeper?

Fairies can be drained eventually, and would die. Keepers, especially children, have so much energy, that they would give him enough to break free. I'm surprised that he hasn't tried for another Keeper. It is a good thing that the Fairy Queen and you freed Jordan when you did. The shadow maze had him so trapped that he could feed enough power eventually to Balkazaar to free him.

But this new tactic is less noticeable. Fairies going missing are not as noticed as a Keeper. We can feel where you are trapped, but unless shielded like Jordan was in the Shadow Maze, most of the time Keepers are easy to find.

I took a moment. Maybe because it was so simple, but I thought suddenly of what we could do. This was much more dangerous than what happened to me during the summer. After all, the only thing I had to do was find healing water and free a Fairy Queen. Now, I could be trapped like Jordan.

But then I wondered what would happen if he didn't have the fairies trapped. "Can we free the fairies? Is there a way to destroy the box?"

The Green Man held his chin in thought. He almost looked like a tree; he was sitting so still. He quietly asked me, "Do you want to help free the fairies Wanda? Do you want to help them?"

No, it's too dangerous. You can't ask her to do that. Brewford started to wag his tail in his irritated twitch.

"What's too dangerous? You could at least tell me." This time I didn't hesitate to put my hands on my hips. "You say I'm a powerful Keeper. You can at least tell me what it is that's so dangerous about it. I might be able to really help free them."

At least her confidence has grown. Castrotomas nodded. He got a wise Yoda look on his face again. *It's the confidence you will need for this mission. It may be the greatest challenge you'll face as a Keeper.*

I waited for the answer. The pause was interrupted with an irritated Brewford. *You can't ask her to do it. No, Castro No. She's not ready. She hasn't come that far in her studies.*

Castrotomas interrupted with a calming tone. *There is nothing better for training than hands on experience. It may be the only way Master Brewford. She will have to meet Balkazaar and face him.*

But only a Keeper can break the spell freeing the fairies, and when she does, he'll feel it breaking. Brewford was sounding really stressed out. *She isn't full in her power to face him. It's too risky.*

"Who says I can't do it?" I started to feel the confidence now. "Besides, you don't always have to stay around. Sometimes you have to know when to run and retreat. I can run fast. Maybe the best way would be to sneak in and get out fast. That's usually the best way on TV."

Brewford looked at me; nose up. *"Well, sometimes TV doesn't always have the best advice. It is still very dangerous."*

I snapped my fingers after an "A-ha" thought. " Maybe I can use the ley lines or something? Can a unicorn guide me? Are they faster than a dark sorcerer?" Sometimes I can feel that light bulb in my head turn on.

It is true. The unicorn Chyra might be able to get in and out faster than Balkazaar. Castrotomas perked up. *She is the swiftest of her kind.*

"Cool! Sounds like you're out-voted Brew." He stared me down with an "I'll talk with you later" look. Cats always hate to lose an argument. He was going to be impossible later.

I ignored the Brew and said to Castro, "So, where is the quickest way to find a unicorn?"

CHAPTER 12

Riding the Paths

So there I was. I was climbing onto the back of a unicorn, again, not sure of what was going to happen. Let alone I didn't know where we should go. At least I knew what I was supposed to do. I just didn't know where or how it would all turn out. Yeah, no problem, right?

Good luck Keeper Wanda, Castro stood up straighter as his head voice resounded in my mind. We were outside his hovel-like tree house.

"Remember, luck can go a long way Wanda." The Green Man's voice boomed with warmth.

Just remember to come back. The Ley Lines can be a confusing place, and I might.... Brewford stopped in his thought speech and sighed. *...I will miss you far too much if you do not come back.*

"I'll be fine Brew. I'll come back, don't worry." I straightened up and got a firm grip on the mane. I felt like I was riding into the sunset like any hero off to save the world. Then again, maybe there was something to stories that had the hero going off like that. It did lift your spirits if you were the hero.

Castro's mind speech interrupted my thoughts. *There is a great risk in riding the Ley Lines Wanda. Some people can wander for years and only return to the Real World to find all their loved ones old or gone forever. Heed what Chyra says. Never get off her back. She is the one who knows the Ley Lines the best. When you reach the cave you saw in the crystal, do not stray far from Chyra. She is a lifeline in the Lines of Power. Unicorns are your steady rock in the stream.*

I nodded and turned Chyra around. The unicorn lowered her horn and a small blue spark shot off. It stopped before us and grew into a wide oval of light that swirled within.

Be careful after entering the door to the Ley Lines, added Brew. *It might be bumpy for we are near a vortex of power. Just ride the currents.*

"And you may need this." The Green Man tossed me a black velvet bag. "Inside is the crystal sphere. It should guide you to the cave you saw. Just tell Chyra what you see and the unicorn should be able to sense the energies along the paths. Good luck to you again Keeper."

I bowed to the Green Man. I nodded to Brewford and Castrotomas. "I'll find them and set them free. Balkazaar won't even know I'm there, until it's too late."

I carefully took the crystal out of the bag and looked into it. I could see the cave with shamrocks and clover growing around the entrance. It looked similar to the cave on the Irish Beach when I first arrived. "That looks really familiar. Can you sense the energy path, Chyra?"

"Yes Keeper. Let us begin."

I wish I could tell you I felt like the brave heroine going off to save the day. My trusty sword would be waving above my head as the unicorn stood up to do a triumphant rearing back stand on it's hind legs.

But that's not how I felt. In fact, I had a huge swarm of the butterflies invading my stomach. I was feeling like I'd just gone for a long car ride, and needed some air. I guess in a nutshell; I was feeling darn scared. Fear is not what I expected to feel as a hero.

I mean it seemed brave at first as an idea, going in and grabbing the fairies. But then all the factors of what could go wrong started to hit me. What if he appeared and I couldn't get out fast? What if he caught me? What would the Dark Sorcerer do?

I was trying not to think too deeply on the subject. If I did, I think it would have been a panic attack for certain. Instead I concentrated on hanging onto the back of the unicorn. If I balanced wrong, I could feel the sway of her walk tilting me to one side. I mean, being afraid was making me a bit dizzy. If I fell off, then nothing would get done. I had to do something. After all, I was a Keeper now.

"So, what do we do first Chyra?" I held the rein just up a bit, trying to use every Western Movie image engrossed in my brain to help me ride. "How do we find him?"

Just look into the sphere and direct me Wanda. Her encouraging tone bolstered my mood. *The crystal sphere should help us trace his energy through the paths. Look into the crystal and tell me what you see.*

I retrieved the crystal sphere from the black velvet bag again. I held it up to my right eye and looked through. Streams of light danced in different directions. A ray of dark blue went sideways by me, followed by another streak of red.

"How do I know which one is his energy?"

Chyra looked about. *What were the colors you saw coming out of the cave where the fairies were trapped?*

"They were green sparks, almost a neon green."

Look for those through the crystal. They'll draw us right to him.

Just as she said it, I saw a neon bolt of green dash off to my left.

"Left," I hollered pointing towards the direction of the green bolt. Then it twitched down another corridor. "Wait, now right."

Good, I think we're on the trail now. She started to pick up speed to a canter. I wobbled back and forth trying to get my riding legs again as the green sparks turned again. This time, it moved in a diagonal right.

"Quick, it just did a right."

She started to a faster trot. "Now right again."

My directions picked up as the bolt started to speed up. Unicorns could move fast, but energy was faster. "Quicker! We're loosing it! I'm losing sight of it behind corners."

Not for long! Chyra's determined voice echoed in my mind as the edges of the corridor started to glide by at a blinding pace.

"Go left now." I was starting to lose track of time. It was all down to following this green bolt of energy through the crystal. "Again left."

Up ahead I saw the bolt dive downward into a dark area. "It dove down now."

It's exiting into the Real World. Hold on, this might be a bit bumpy.

Bumpy was an understatement. It was like riding your favorite roller coaster with horsehair. The exit was like going through one of the tunnels that is fun to scream in. I didn't scream. There was no sound of anything. No trot of the unicorn's hooves. No swish of the bolts travel. Then we were in a forest, dodging trees as the bolt skidded around them. "Chyra, we're going to lose it."

No we're not. I've never had any energy force outrun me yet.

I think she could see it now, because it glowed a bit even when I wasn't using the crystal. It was brighter when I held it up, but when I took it down, I could still see it.

"Ouch!" I ducked to avoid a branch, but still got a face full of leaves and twigs. "Chyra, try to look out for trees?"

Sorry Keeper. Chasing a bolt of energy does make it hard to navigate obstacles. Energy tends to speed up when they return to their source. Look, it just dodged to the right. I think we're almost there.

I could hear the thunder of her hooves now. I just held onto the mane. It helped me to feel secure on her back. Things around me were a blur now, with much of the forest in a dim, grayish light. It must be twilight now. It would be nighttime soon.

HOLD ON!

Chyra jumped over some fallen logs and I balanced with her motion. We landed in-step with her natural rhythm. It was like riding a river. I just flowed with her movement.

Chyra's mind speech broke into my concentration. *You okay, Wanda?*

"Yes, I'm still here. I think."

I laid low to her back as we continued pursuit. The pounding of my heart matched her hoof beats. Then I saw the bolt disappear into a large opening in the rocks. It had to be the cave.

Chyra slowed to a stop. *I think we're here.*

I gave her a pat on the neck. "Yeah, and now I guess it's up to me."

CHAPTER 13

Meeting Old Friends

I slid off of Chyra's back near the entrance to the cave. It looked like it did in the crystal, except the entrance was a black gape.

I turned to her and saw one indigo eye watching me. I voiced my concern. "I feel like we're making this up as we go". There, that helped put things into perspective.

We usually do. She nudged me forward with her nose as I looked at the dark entrance. *The best way to get started is forward.*

"I think I've heard that somewhere before," I said after looking back at her. I started to stroke her nose. Her coat was so soft, almost cat-like. "Now that I'm here, it's not as easy to be brave."

Bravery is never easy. Just know it's what you've got to do. Don't think more than that.

I gave her a pat. "Could you follow behind me, just in case?"

Of course, but remember to trust in yourself. Your friends are there for support, but in the end, it all comes down to you.

"I will."

I looked again at the opening. I'd been in dark caves before. But often I was more curious. It felt like an adventure back when I was exploring the crystal cave, being lead by my friend Brownie, Malik. It's how I became a Keeper.

But maybe it was the fear of the unknown. What was in the cave after all? Sometimes it's adventure, and sometimes it's just scary. I was trying to decide what it was. It's best to choose the adventure side.

"One step forward seems to work the best," I thought out loud. I looked down at my feet, and willed them forward. I concentrated on getting one to go first, than the other. My crystal pendant started to glow as I entered the cave. The friendly warmth seeped through my t-shirt reminding me of the crystal fairy always with me.

Her metallic voice tingled through my mind. *Remember, that chaos is the beginning of finding oneself.*

I took a deep breath. "Better to face your fears. That's what the elves said during my summer training." I looked down again. "Let's go feet."

Chyra moved forward to take the lead. *Let me go first. I'll scout ahead.*

With a dip of her horn, she started to move into the darkness. As soon as we were far enough in the cave opening, her horn sprang to life with light. The cave chamber shot into vivid reality. A large circle of stones was at its center. Fireflies danced within the circle with dead bee bodies strewn about the outside of the stones.

Careful Wanda. This could still be a trap. Chyra's thoughts echoed my own. I might only be 11, but I'd played enough video games to realize that rushing forward into any level was entirely stupid.

I walked forward cautiously, keeping a watch around me. It looked harmless, but that sometimes seems to be the trick to most traps. It's part of the disguise.

As I walked around the circle, I noticed tiny fireflies dancing in the middle. The crunch of dead bees underfoot creeped me out. Then, I started to hear small voices. My crystal pendant got warm on my shirt. So I grabbed it. I was learning the crystal fairy had something to say that way. The warmer the crystal pendant, the more urgent the message. This time when I touched it her bell voice rang more urgently than ever. *Be careful, the Shadow Lord is sure to be about.*

Then the voices in the circle of stones got louder. "Help us Keeper, help us." The fireflies seemed to be hovering right in front of my face. It was like talking to dancing tiny moths of light. "Danger if you approach us." "Save yourself before it's too late."

The last comment got me to thinking maybe it would be a good idea to leave. Nothing had happened yet. Maybe I was lucky so far. Why try to push my luck? If I backed off nice and easy; nothing would happen. I'd be safe. I started to walk a little backwards.

I shook myself. It had to be a mind trap. Last time I'd engaged in one of these, it was in the shadow maze when I helped Jordan, the last Keeper, to escape. Seemed that whenever you got closer to solving things, someone always set a mind trap.

I started to block the doubt and fight the mind trap's influence. Logic was a good way to fight it. But the thoughts kept jumping into my brain. Think logical. I tried to imagine myself as Spock. I guess it was just too much Star Trek movies while at my Dad's house. But it did work. I distanced myself from the doubt, and it faded.

I circled the stones again with the fireflies following in a group with me. They seemed to shadow my path, like they were watching. Were these the missing fairies? They looked like creatures of some sort, but I couldn't make them out through the green tinted walls that surrounded the stones. Maybe if I had something to throw at the circle, I could trigger the trap. It would be like poking a stick in a mousetrap.

I looked around on the ground. Several stones were a good throwing size. But I didn't want to hit the fairies trapped in the stone circle. Chyra followed my direction and lit my path while I searched. There. A small twig might do it.

I picked it up and dashed back to the outside of the stone circle. I held my breath as I threw the twig. The green light wall flared suddenly and burned it to a cinder. Thought so. It had been too easy so far. There's always a catch.

"So, how do we get them out Chyra?"

"You can't," boomed a familiar voice. The smell of a cat box not changed for weeks wafted at me. The man I'd met on the beach trail materialized as if from a fog. It was very transporter beam like, an appearance from nowhere. It was a bit unnerving, especially when he smiled right at me. His perfect teeth grin still made me uneasy.

OK, I thought. So much for surprise. The sneaking in and out plan was out the window. Now what? I hadn't thought of a Plan B. Oops. I wasn't a prepared heroine after all.

He was standing less than three feet from the circle, the smile turning into a glare. "We have a lot to finish, you and I. Too bad I didn't have the chance the last time we met." He smiled again, with a wicked twist to his lips. "I've been waiting a long time for you to find me. Finally, I'll have what I'll need." Again, there was the steady smile.

"Well." I eyed him back with a challenge in my voice similar to Bruce Willis. I folded my arms too, and tried to stand straighter. I raised my eyebrow as well. A little attitude wasn't going to hurt. "And what have you needed so badly, Shadow Sorcerer Balkazaar?" I tried to slow his name a bit like I was in a movie.

"Good. You do know who I am." He took a bow. "Sorry I couldn't go through formal introduction when we last met. It would have ruined my element of surprise." He grinned as the smell of rank garbage assaulted my nose.

"The Fairy Queen has told me about you, and so has the Green Man." I tried to sound tough and not afraid.

He chuckled. "Long time friends." He chuckled again. "Sometimes it's the friends that know you the most that can hurt you back. Am I what you imagined? I hope I live up to your expectations." He started to twist his thin, black mustache. Then, he smiled with a smirk.

"They're not big fans of you. So, they didn't really give a lot of details, except that you're really, really bad." It was my turn to smile.

He full out laughed now. "You are an interesting adversary Keeper. I haven't found any challenge such as you for centuries. I do hope that our time is not so limited, for I am enjoying the…" He eyed me slowly. "match up."

"Luckily, I only need one Keeper to harness the power to break free," he continued. "And if you won't do, than I will find someone else." This time his smile was more akin to evil overlord in most movies. You know, the bad guy thinks he can always win type. He went back to twisting his mustache.

Suddenly, he pointed to the wall. An oval shaped vortex of light appeared on the wall beside him. Yellow and green light swirled to form a clear-like mirror. It changed as I looked into a scene of trees and grass. Then a figure appeared in the scene. It was like watching television, until the figure started running towards me.

"Wanda, Wanda! Where have you been the last two days?" It was Eddie's voice. She came into focus as she ran towards us. I saw her red hair bouncing as she ran, arms pumping at her sides as she tried to reach the spot where I was standing. Except I knew it was a trap, but not for me. It was for Eddie.

"NO, Eddie! Don't!" I tried to put my hands up to signal stop. But she came bounding through the oval opening. "Wanda, there you are. I've been waiting here for two hours after school. What's up? We were supposed to meet. That's what your note said."

"I didn't write a note Eddie." A laugh echoed behind us.

She headed towards me right into another stone circle. A green wall of light sprung up around her. She reached out to touch the edges and jumped back sucking her fingertips. She started to shout at me, but I could hear nothing.

"So now you have to make a choice." Balkazaar's voice boomed through out the cave chamber. "Do you save your friend or do you save the fairies? Which ever you choose, I still win." His laughter echoed off the cave walls.

CHAPTER 14

Choices

Why does the bad guy always do that? The villain always likes to get the hero stuck in some tough decision. I started to remember what my grandmother had taught me when she showed me the card game of Bridge. I was probably the only 9 year old that liked to jump up and down if she played a trump card. And here Balkazaar had delivered an ultra trump card. He trapped Eddie, my new friend, right under my nose. So now what do I do?

I felt cornered, but not defeated. Defeated was not in my vocabulary. There had to be something he'd missed. That's how it worked. The bad guy misses something, and the hero figures out what it is and then, bam. Cue the theme music. Mental note, I needed some theme music for times like this. So, now, what did he miss?

"I don't have all day Wanda. It's time to choose who you will save." He pointed to the fairies. "The Pillywiggins...". He pointed to the green walled column with Eddie with her arms folded. "...Or your friend."

Eddie had the most miffed look on her face. I didn't blame her. I would have hated to be tricked like that. And she'd been a Keeper longer than me. When I looked at her, I saw her mouth slowly...F-air-ries.

I took a moment. Hmm. Television did come in handy sometimes. Sometimes the best way to figure a solution is to buy yourself some time. That's what they always did when they had more of the hour to fill. So I thought quickly.

"You wouldn't want to give any hints on how to save them would you?" He raised an eyebrow so I continued. "I was still working on how to save the fairies when you interrupted with the friend trapping over there. If I'm going to make a choice, then I should at least know how to save one. It would be only fair."

He started laughing. "It would be no fun to make it too easy. But I have to say a good effort of playing your move. I could tell you how to free at least one, and then it would make your choice extra hard."

He lowered his voice. "But I don't think you've discovered the trick to being a Keeper. So I'm going to wait and see what your choice would be first. That should make it all more interesting. Than we'll talk about how to get them out."

Oh well. So much for getting the bad guy to tell me his plan when he thought he'd won. That's what happened in tons of movies, not just TV. But books were always having trick endings. Score one for literature. I wonder what Balkazaar's trick was?

He eyed me coldly. "So who will it be?"

What was Balkazaar's trick? There had to be something I was missing.

My pendant got warm. I grabbed it quickly hoping Balkazaar wouldn't notice. *Sometimes the wanting and wishing are so obvious that most Keepers miss the connection. They are much the same.*

Balkazaar muttered. "Stop stalling. I don't have all day."

I still couldn't make up my mind. Questions bought time. My pendant started to grow warm again. I held it and heard the crystal fairy's familiar voice: *Remember what the Fairy Queen told you about wishing when you first met her.*

I shook my head and whispered back, "No, I don't remember what the Queen said about wishing."

Eddie began jumping up and down. She mouthed "Wishing-is-ma-gic."

Wishing, what did Eddie mean? Then I remembered what the Fairy Queen had said. It echoed in my brain as if the Queen was standing right next to me. "Sometimes, a wish is strong enough to overcome the hardest obstacle."

It's like a light bulb went on in my head. "A wish can solve my problem?"

The Crystal Fairy added to my thought. *Magic isn't just a wish, but the will to have it be your goal.*

"Like wishing for something and figuring a way to make it happen?"

The Shadow Sorcerer chuckled. "Very good Wanda. Sounds like your studies are coming right along. Let me help you." He sneered and the green walls around both the fairies and Eddie started to move inward. "Choose. Now."

Help. What was it Brewford said about help? I clung to that word as the clue I'd been looking for.

Sometimes a Keeper has to remember when to ask for help. The Crystal Fairy echoed her advice. I looked at Balkazaar sneering. Time was running out.

But who can a person ask for help when things are going against you?

I looked at Edina, my new friend and fellow Keeper. A friend. Friends are there to help. They're someone you can count on. Wait. She was a Keeper too, and could also make a wish.

My choice became a decision. It was one of those moments when you feel your destiny. You can sense the change within you as you follow a dream or figure a solution to a problem. I mouthed back to Eddie, "A-fter-me-wish." She nodded.

Then I said clearly, "I wish to free my friend Eddie so she can free the fairies."

There was a loud pop. Eddie's wall swirled and blew apart hitting the walls with a large blast of air. She looked like a hairdryer had blown her hair outward for at least 30 minutes, while plastering it with hairspray the whole time.

Then Eddie began her wish, "I wish for the Pillywiggin Fairies to be free from their trap."

There was another loud pop. The Pillywiggin Fairies blew out from the green surrounding walls and swarmed around the cave. They swarmed around us both like fireflies. I started to giggle as Eddie walked towards me. "Thanks Wanda. That was quick thinking. It's always a good idea for Keepers to work together." She held out her hand.

I put out my hand and shook her hand. "Not just Keepers, friends."

"Yeah, friends. You know, we got to work on that secret hand shake."

She was still shaking my hand when Balkazaar said, "This is not over yet, Keepers." It all happened at once. One moment Eddie was standing in front of me with her big smile, and strange hairdo. The next, Balkazaar was flying across the cave sweeping her straight off her feet into a whirlwind of green light. She screamed, and it echoed off the walls. It was all that was left of her and Balkazaar. They both disappeared into a large tornado that erupted in the center of the cave. It spun to a single point and was gone.

The last thing I heard from them was Balkazaar's voice echoing off the walls of the cave. "We will meet again, I promise." And then he was gone, with Eddie.

Stunned disbelief hit me like an avalanche. How could I miss that move? I thought I was pretty good at games. I thought I'd won, and then he just takes Eddie.

"It's not fair. I won fair and square. I figured a way. Eddie and I had beaten him."

Chyra came over and nuzzled my hand. *No it's not. Life is not fair. People live by their choices. You chose to work with your friend, and she wished to save the fairies. It was a solution with teamwork.*

She snorted before she continued. *But Balkazaar chose to not accept the choice. He made a choice for himself. And it's not fair. Dark Sorcerer's are rarely fair. It's what makes them dark in the first place.*

I hung my head. "I totally failed this one. I suck as a Keeper."

Chyra touched her horn to my forehead. "Do not feel so. You have saved the Pillywiggin Fairies. You found out why our allies, the honeybees, were being killed. You did not fail. For now, all are safe until Balkazaar tries again. The battle will just continue another day. And it is now time to return home."

Some of the Pillywiggins came over and hovered in front of me. I tried to avoid them by looking down. They hovered underneath and tickled my nose. A whole chorus of them sang at once, "Thank you Keeper."

I looked over at Chyra's purple-blue eyes. A gentle, relaxed feeling passed over me. Her head voice continued the soothing feeling. *Some battles have outcomes that are not planned. But you can't ignore the good that you have done already. Come; let us ride the paths back to your bedchamber. Your mother will be worried.*

I swung up onto Chyra and she exited the cave. A portal of light opened in front of us, and we entered the paths. Again, I saw the crystals along the path, the water and passages. But I didn't pay much attention. I was feeling like I'd failed.

I know heroes were not supposed to sulk, but I couldn't help it. I felt like I'd let Eddie down. Here I'd finally made a friend with another Keeper, and I'd messed it up. She was gone. It was worse than having Michelle move away. I felt responsible. And I didn't know why Balkazaar had taken her. It scared me to think of what he might be thinking of doing with her.

His words that he needed a Keeper to break through to our world came rushing back. I sat up on Chyra making her stop suddenly. "Oh no. I think he needs Eddie to help him escape to our world." I'd been warned that being a Keeper was dangerous, but here it was first hand. I didn't realize it might be dangerous for others. "He could use her powers to escape."

We will find your friend. Chyra looked back at me. *With our allies, we can stop the Shadow Sorcerer, somehow. We just need time.*

I sighed. "Nothing left but to ride into the sunset or at least the rest of the way home, I guess."

We are almost to your bedchamber, answered Chyra. *Plus, unicorns cannot ride into the sun. Rainbows though, are no problem.*

I laughed a little. I started to relax the rest of the way home on the paths. Maybe it wasn't going to be so bad. All I had to do was go home, and figure someway to find Eddie again. There had to be a way to save her.

"Let's hurry Chyra. I'm sure Mom will be mad if I'm not home soon. Who knows how late it is in the real world? Eddie said she hadn't seen me for two days. I think my middle name is going to be grounded." I snapped my fingers as I had my next thought. "Think the fairies can fold a little time back for me? Though it might be nice to miss the Social Studies Quiz I have today."

Chyra nodded as we walked near the end of another passage. *I will follow a path that will lead us back to your room two days earlier. This will allow you more time to study for this, Social Studies Test, correct?* Suddenly, another light portal appeared before us, there was a bit of a flash. And then I was in my room, sitting on Chyra.

I slipped off her back, and threw myself onto my bed. The fact I was finally home helped me forget some of the situation.

I sighed. "Home. Maybe Dorothy had the right idea of not wanting to go anywhere but stay home." I lay back in my bed. I heard someone walking down the hall. I looked to see Chyra leaving through the light portal.

Her last thoughts echoed in my mind. *Remember you are a Keeper. You will think of a way to find Eddie. And you will do fine on your Social Studies Test. You still have two days. Good luck Keeper.*

The door opened just as the portal disappeared. Mom stood in the doorway leaning her head in. "Up sleepy head. Oh, I see you are up. Well, that's the best way to start the day, looking ready."

"Yeah Mom. Didn't want to waste any time today." And a best friend to find. I didn't say that part out loud of course. But I knew in the back of my mind I was going to find a way to find Eddie. There had to be a way to rescue her, even if I had to search the whole world to find her. And I would too. I had to. She was my friend.

I got up and went through the door to get ready for school. Brewford stepped through the door. His tail twitched as he gave me a stern look. *Where have you been? I've been worried sick. I just managed to catch up after that last time jump. Unicorns are so direct in their travel. Sometimes they are hard to keep up with.*

"You were following me?" I asked suspicious.

Only after we felt the release of the fairies Wanda. That much transfer of power was felt by all of the Cat Sorcerers and most likely, several Crystal Keepers. But let us go have some breakfast. There is much work to do, and I never like to work on an empty stomach.

"Most cats don't Brew."

I opened the door and started to follow Brewford to get some breakfast. After all, a Keeper's work is important work and not easy to do on an empty stomach. I looked at Brewford as he headed down the hall. After all, I had Brewford, the fairies, and even a unicorn now to help me find Edina. And if it was a school day; a Keeper has to make sure she keeps her grades up. I headed to the kitchen table and poured myself a bowl of cereal. Time to face the future.

Join Wanda in her next adventure, <u>The Lost Secret of Dragonfire</u> as she tries to find her friend and fellow Keeper Edina. Her journey will take her to other Fairy Worlds where she will enlist the help of the Dwarves and the Menehunes, the Hawaiian fairies. Not to mention, some help from those elusive Time Masters, the Dragons.

For more information about the author and other Crystal Keeper Chronicle books, please visit the author's website at: http://<u>www.tiffmeister.net/writer.html</u>

Want a crystal pendant just like a Keeper? Send in the coupon below, and receive your very own, hand-made crystal pendant. Cut out and send the coupon with $2.95 for shipping to:

Tiffany Turner
Crystal Keeper Pendant
6081 Meridian Ave. Ste.70
Box 116
San Jose, CA 95120

You will receive an official Keeper Certificate signed by the author, Tiffany Turner and Fairy Queen Lillith. If you have already signed up as an official Crystal Keeper, Queen Lillith is guarding your membership. Wear your crystal proudly. *This offer is for first time Crystal Keepers only.

Name: _____

Address: _____

_____

_____

Would you like information on other Crystal Keeper Chronicle

Books? Yes or No   Please circle

Printed in the United States
by Baker & Taylor Publisher Services